Black Light Void

Dark Visions of the Caribbean

EDITED BY MARSHA PEARCE

HANSIB

First published in Great Britain by Hansib Publications in 2023

Hansib Publications Limited
76 High Street, Hertford, SG14 3TA, United Kingdom

info@hansibpublications.com
www.hansibpublications.com

Publication of this book was made possible in part by a generous grant from the University of the West Indies Campus Research and Publication Fund.

Front cover art: Edward Bowen, *Edge of the White Forest*, acrylics, mixed media on canvas, 72 x 84 inches, 2017. Courtesy of the artist. Photo: Melissa Miller.

ISBN 978-1-7393211-0-9
ISBN 978-1-7393211-1-6 (Kindle)
ISBN 978-1-7393211-2-3 (ePub)

A CIP catalogue record for this book
is available from the British Library

Production by Hansib Publications
Printed in Great Britain

www.hansibpublications.com

For Alexander

CONTENTS

Don't fear the dark...

Black Light Void: Beyond Sunlit Epistemologies

Marsha Pearce

It is hot in the tropics. This is not knowledge gleaned from travel magazines, with their sun-drenched images. Having been born and raised in the twin-island state of Trinidad and Tobago, it is an assertion of lived fact. Beyond oscillations between the dry and rainy seasons, I rarely check the day's temperature. Heat is, for the most part, a constant. There is little need to verify small shifts in degrees. Instead, it is the modulation of light that draws my attention – the progression of soft morning light to the piercing afternoon sun arcing across minutes, hours, before slipping into that pocket where sky meets earth. Light's brightness changes. Its angles vary. In reading its qualities I note the way its shape also morphs: how it narrows between fig leaves, or swells as it bounces off vehicles in downtown traffic. Light's condition is fickle. Yet, what is often unchanging is its warmth. This is not evidence of a feverish state, but the recognition of a visual sensation. Impressions of yellows, oranges and even pink light make heat a phenomenon that is not only felt in the tropics, but seen. Acts of seeing, however, are never neutral. There are implications of such sight. While we might argue that light changes everywhere, what is at stake in reading light's colour is not making critical connections between its hotter hues, or cooler tones, and the specificities of place – not seeing the link to how we experience and understand a particular place, and ourselves, through colour.

According to insights from light psychology, we relax in places illuminated by warm, yellow light. In contrast, contexts lit by cool, bluish light help us to see clearly – they are spaces of attentiveness and deep concentration. Light's colour temperature has a psychic effect on us. What this means for the tropics is expressed in Derek Walcott's comparison of hot and cold geographic locations. "For tourists, the sunshine cannot be serious," he observes, while "winter adds depth and darkness to life" (1998: p. 72). In places historically defined in terms of a leisure and pleasure trope, bodies loosen up, minds calm and the gaze relaxes. Seeing is reduced to the clichés of sea, sand and palm tree. Under the warm sunlight, experiential nuances are often overlooked by the traveller in search of a tropical escape. Fluid details are missed in a perpetual, amber heat. What if we removed colour from the psychic equation that sums up a sense of place? What if tropical places could be seen in a different light?

This book, with its focus on the Caribbean, attends to what it means to see in the dark. It considers darkness or, more specifically, blackness as a critical epistemic space for seeing place and identity. It pushes a discourse about easy, transparent readings of the Other – facile interpretations of the Caribbean – beyond a proposal to see in terms of opacity. It moves from the opaque to the dark; from what Glissant calls "le droit à l'opacité" (1997: p.29), the right to opacity, to a right to darkness. It situates its discussion and contents within a discourse on Caribbean aesthetics, taking the word aesthetic from the Greek term *aisthesthai*, to "perceive." What is addressed, therefore, is the matter of perception and knowledge in and of the Caribbean, and the selves that engage it. I posit critical aesthetic practices are not those readily seen, they are not those enacted in the sun – the visible light that is a defining feature of the tropics – but in the dark. I argue for seeing and reading the Caribbean in the dark.

A Different Illumination

This work is concerned with a nuanced space: what I refer to as the black light void, a space beyond the horizon of what we already know, or think we know; beyond assumptions, stereotypes and the taken-for-granted. Beyond what sunlight renders visible. It is a space with a different illumination. In this space there are no reds, no burnt siennas or saffron yellows, no cobalt blues or indigos. Colour is not a factor. Black is the absence of colour, the absence of visible light. The black light void emits an invisible UV light to make new visibilities possible, that is, it induces or brings about what I call an *ultravisuality* – a radical, unpredictable way of seeing. A type of sight that engages the *unlooked-for*. In the black light void, luminescence is given to what is present – to what is there – but not readily discerned. In the black light void, things glow in the dark. Forms emerge. Black as metaphor, rather than colour with its attendant psychological burdens, gestures toward psychic freedom; a liberty to see something else.

The black light void is both a theory of sight and a praxis. It is the deliberate work of going to the edge of our awareness, leaving behind incandescent visions, to leap into a space in which the light source is our imagination. By imagination, I do not mean the imaginary, or the fictive, but rather, imagination as an *act* embedded in the real, as *actuality* – "imagination as a social practice" (Appadurai, 1996: p.31) that shapes and is shaped by everyday realities. I am thinking about imagination as:

> No longer mere fantasy (opium for the masses whose real work is elsewhere), no longer simple escape (from a world defined principally by more concrete purposes and structures), no longer elite pastime (thus not relevant to the lives of ordinary people), and no longer mere contemplation (irrelevant for new forms of desire and subjectivity)... (Ibid.)

but as that which confronts the real and attends to our daily circadian rhythms, in constructions of our being. Imagination is an optical force for seeing what has been concealed, suppressed, neglected. It is a re-membering of lived experiences. Imagination is a critical generator of light in the black light void, a light that bends around formulas of existence, one cast outside the fixities and finitudes ascribed to places and people. This light falls on the unseen, giving it dimension and volume: a curve, a crevice, an edge. In this way, it sculpts and conjures the unnoticed, bringing it into consciousness, where there is potential to process, refine and redraft how we picture our complex world and ourselves. The black light void is a shift to the unpopular imagination.

This space of radical sight, the void, is "empty" insofar as we do not occupy it. We cannot inhabit it with any permanence. Once we project our minds into the void, we expand the territory of our awareness. We find ourselves back in our solar sanctums, with their already familiar landscapes. Taking what we perceive in the void, we can mould new peaks and valleys, transforming the vistas of our being. But all new compositions become worn and obvious over time. In the sun's glare, we can get blind spots – areas of limited sight. As praxis, therefore, the black light void is recursive. It requires our return to its epistemic infinity (can we ever know everything about our vast and changing world?) to enlarge our self-understanding and broaden our positionality in place and time. Such returns reanimate the eye. They keep us from relaxing our gaze and submitting to the seductions of warm light.

Beyond our presumptions, the void is free of our meanings, our human interpretations, but it is not a vacant space. Its forms are latent. They exist imaginatively. Yet, it is precisely because the void can appear empty and sense-less – outside of our sensory experience – that it can elicit a fear of the unknown and the unknowable. The void, appearing as a gaping maw, threatens to swallow us whole. Our minds, therefore, are not always open to the journey. Yet, Caribbean people know something about being consumed; our cultures, human bodies and natural environment have been devoured by the West, for centuries (Sheller, 2003). Today, we remain in the jaw of colonialism's after-effects, having clawed our way out of its belly. At the heart of that clawing process is the light of the imagination, shone on our shadowed subjectivities: "the exercise of that creative imagination has remained a major instrument of liberation in the Caribbean... [and] the Caribbean creative artist has been in the vanguard of a genuine cultural revolution" (Nettleford, 2003: pp. 165-166). This book chronicles a group of artists – both visual and literary – from the English-speaking Caribbean, who dare to venture into the black light void.

Let Us Imagine Together: Ekphrasis as Collaboration and as Creole

The title of the book is taken from Edward Bowen, a Caribbean contemporary artist noted for his contribution to the birth of an alternative art scene in the early 90s, in Trinidad. He may be described as what writer and critic, Annie Paul tentatively refers to as an "alter *native*," that is, an artist in the Caribbean context who is "not interested in...promoting and supporting national agendas" (2003: n.pag.). Alter *natives* are artists "with unpopular narratives. Often their talent is recognized abroad before it is accepted at home" (ibid.). Paul observes that Bowen's images are distinguished by a refusal of insertion "into the Anglophone Caribbean's prevailing paradigm of aesthetic nationalism" (2006: n.pag.). His work is a counterpoint to nostalgic, romanticised depictions of ordinary life – subjects, which preoccupied the majority of Caribbean nationalist schools (Poupeye, 1988: p.53).

In November 2017, Bowen exhibited a series of large-scale paintings in *Stories*, his solo show held at Y Art Gallery, Trinidad. For the written documentation accompanying his artworks, Bowen opted to pen his reflections on his process and experiences as a local image-maker. In thinking about his approach to painting, he shared:

> ...the mind wants a story of predictable intent; the mind does not want to go too far, if at all, into that black light void, where form is not seen or anticipated... but like a writer wants to write a new story, I want to paint a new story.

Bowen voices a tendency to move toward familiar forms and preconceived themes in the narratives we tell. Our stories of place and people often carry expected beginnings, middles and endings. In opposition, Bowen advocates for something unforeseeable. He wants to paint a new story, an impetus he takes up using his locatedness in the Caribbean (all stories start somewhere) as a medium. What stories lie beyond sunlight? Beyond the sun-kissed, stock image of tropical islands? I address these questions by way of Bowen's paintings from that 2017 exhibition, and the work of six Trinidadian writers: Kevin Jared Hosein, Barbara Jenkins, Sharon Millar, Amílcar Sanatan, Portia Subran and Elizabeth Walcott-Hackshaw, who accepted my invitation to create short stories *in response* to his images.

The word "response" is important to this book, which takes an ekphrastic form. In considering what it means to respond to something, I am deploying a notion of ekphrasis in rhetorical, rather than representational terms. Traditional theories of ekphrasis approach it as writing that imitates or describes a visual work. However, the idea is invoked here as a sensory reaction or perception. Ekphrasis is understood as "a performative gesture"; emphasis is given to "the performative instead of the mimetic" (Brosch, 2018: pp. 226 & 227). As performance, I am interested in the cultural function of ekphrasis – in what it can do, and with what effects. By situating ekphrasis within the cultural context of the Caribbean a parallel can be drawn between its practice, and the call-and-response compositions known as the lavway. With its roots in traditional African music, the lavway is a chant that is conversational in form. A singer calls, the audience responds, and vice versa. Historical accounts note the word's phonetic derivation from a French colonial influence on language in the Caribbean region. Lavway is said to have come from *le vrai*, the French word meaning "the truth" (Pemberton et al., 2018), or *la voix*, which translates to "the voice" (Warner, 1982).

By understanding ekphrasis as a Caribbean lavway, I make room for several voices and many truths. I propose a process in which the artists and the readers of this book participate democratically, as performers of meaning. In this form of ekphrasis, power is decentred: Bowen's artworks constitute his *reactions* to his environment, the short stories offer *perceptions* of the paintings, and the reader is *called* to this performance with her own sensory *responses* to image and word. The book, therefore, is not a space of description, but a space of critical performance. What this means for the Caribbean is a reframing of how we see and make sense of place; a Caribbean perceived by way of dialogic interaction as opposed to a dominant, imperial monologue that has long articulated Western viewpoints of formerly, and still, colonised places. It is also a reframing of agency. As lavway, I insist this ekphrasis is distinct from its Western configuration.

Döring notes, ekphrasis is "a major form within the Western canon because its genealogy colludes with the tradition of the epic" (2002: p.171). An early example is found in Homer's epic poem *The Iliad,* a work describing the shield of Achilles. Such epic works, however, promote asymmetries of power. In his study of epic poetry, Quint argues "an ideology of empire" is inscribed in Virgil's *Aeneid*, an ekphrastic work which describes the shield of Aeneas (1993: p. 21). Virgil's work is regarded as a model of subsequent literary genres using ekphrasis – a template that holds a "vision of concentrated power" (Ibid.: p. 12) and carries a topos of "imperial victors" and the "vanquished enemy" who are "born losers – monstrous, demonic, subhuman" (Ibid.: p.11). Exploring ekphrasis in the Caribbean, I resist a framework of conquest and subjugation. I assert ekphrasis as an indigenised, decolonial form, one in which people can imagine together – in which artist and audience are empowered to perceive and shape narratives in collaboration with each other.

Black Light Void is not only about how we see place and power. It also advances a different means for comprehending the visual and the verbal. An ekphrastic approach that is embedded in Caribbeanness, is also creole in nature. Other cultural researchers have made a link between ekphrasis and creolisation. For example, in her book *Visions of Empire in Colonial Spanish American Ekphrastic Writing*, Kathryn Mayers discusses "Creole ekphrases." Mayers declares her use of the term creole refers "not only to white inhabitants of the Americas but also to persons of mixed genetic heritage (*mestizos*) who, by virtue of their economic, linguistic, and geographic circumstances, came to form part of the Spanish American ruling elite" (2012: p. xviii). I am also interested in mixture and hybridity, however, by a creole ekphrasis, I mean a particular fusion of image and word. I take creole "in the Caribbean sense of forging from disparate elements" a new language that can challenge us to "new ways of knowing" (Nettleford, 2003: p.xv).

A creole ekphrasis resists an inclination to view image and word as binary opposites. It defies the convention of reading image and word as two separate eyes which when considered in relation to each other, register forms that can add up to what we call binocular or stereoscopic vision. An easy calculation of one plus one. Instead, a creole ekphrasis behaves and yields nothing like the elements that comprise it. Just as water, a liquid with its own unique properties, is formed from two gases, a creole ekphrasis is a lens that exceeds the union of imaging and writing. It is more than the sum of its parts. What, therefore, might we see with this kind of eye? What is discerned in an advanced arithmetic of painted and worded stories? In experiencing this book, what is perceived in the portals opened by an amalgam of brushstroke and letter stroke? We must read between the marks on the surface of its pages. This book is a site or matrix of perceptions, a hybrid space involving many ways of seeing.

Nothing in the Void

A key dimension of sight in this work is how we see and understand the void in terms of *nothing*. I have proposed that the void is not an empty phenomenon. Building on that proposal, I insist it is a site of nothing. What do I mean? Notions of emptiness and nothing have been variously interpreted within the spheres of creative practice and cultural production. An often-cited example is the work of French artist Yves Klein. In 1958 he presented audiences with an empty white room, apart from a cabinet, at the Iris Clert Gallery in Paris. The exhibition was titled *The Specialisation of Sensibility in the Raw Material State into Stabilised Sensibility*. Historians refer to it as *The Void*. Klein explains his idea behind the work: "I sought to create an ambience, a pictorial climate that is invisible but present" (2007: p.81). He wanted to reintroduce the viewer to matter by challenging what he saw as the tyranny of visible form. Klein's work and that of others such as North American artist Robert Barry's *Closed Gallery* (1969), an exhibition of three shut spaces, and German artist Maria Eichorn's *Wall Text No. 4* (1992), featuring white lettering on a white wall, motivated the show *Voids: A Retrospective* at the Centre Pompidou in 2009. This unconventional museum exhibition offered nine rooms devoid of content, demonstrating nothing's foothold in art history. In 2014, Serbian artist Marina Abramović performed the work *512 Hours* at London's Serpentine Gallery. Abramović spent time with gallery audiences eight hours a day, for 64 days in largely empty spaces. Visitors were asked to store their tablets, phones, watches and other goods in lockers. Speaking about the work, the artist shared:

> What is significant is that *512 Hours* is empty space...When the public comes in...they are arriving to the space with nothing. I am there for them. They are my living material. I am their living material. And from this nothing, something may or may not happen (Serpentine, 2015: n.pag.)

These engagements with the void, reflect various strategies of clearing, emptying or rendering spaces blank as a means of arguing for a presence that remains: put another way, empty space is not empty. Work by Abramović goes further to suggest that nothing has the potential to furnish something; from nothing, "something may or may not happen." It is this generative sense of nothing that I want to highlight here, because it has socio-historical resonance in the Caribbean.

How is *nothing* deployed in Caribbean contexts? Walcott posits a particular relationship to this concept. He asserts: "...deeper than the superficial, existential sense, we in the Caribbean know all about nothing. We know that we owe Europe either revenge or nothing, and it is better to have nothing than revenge. We owe the past revenge or nothing, and revenge is uncreative" (1974: p. 12). Instead of framing nothing in terms of absence and lack, Walcott offers a perspectival antithesis of searing evaluations by those such as nineteenth-century British historian James Anthony Froude and Trinidad-born novelist V.S. Naipaul. During his travels, Froude looked upon the Caribbean islands and saw a nonentity: "there are no people there, in the true sense of the word, with a character and purpose of their own" (1888: p. 347). This sentiment picks up momentum in Naipaul's bleak outlook: "History is built around achievement and creation; and nothing was created in the West Indies" (1962: p.29). Yet, for Walcott, nothing is a creative proposition. According to Jamaican intellectual Edward Baugh, Walcott "sought to transform [nothing] imaginatively from a stigma of non-achievement and hopelessness to an inviting challenge and opportunity" (2006: p. 8). Therefore, to see the void as a site of nothing, is to acknowledge its fertility. As nothing, the void in the Caribbean is aspirational. Unlike the tentative nature of Abramović's statement: "something may or may not happen," the void, as nothing, is a space in which something *will* happen; something *will be created*, if we go to it.

Into the Black Light Void

What does it mean, then, to make something out of nothing – to leave behind presumptions, to imagine something in a void brightened by UV light? Some answers come from my treks to the black light void. I am not exempt from such trips. In formulating this book project, I find my subjectivity intertwined in the call and response. I am part of an ekphrastic performance, a lavway, in which my own meanings are constructed. Close readings of word and image prompt personal visions; a picturing of my lived realities. In *Valley,* Edward Bowen presents two landscape paintings as a diptych. These works reveal bold, diagonal lines open like praying hands now spread apart. In my interpretation of his compositions, I think about the history of the diptych as a visual form used as an altarpiece for devotion. Writer, Barbara Jenkins, reflects on this history, too. In *Hinged*, her short-story response to Bowen's images, she weaves this religious reference as part of her contemplation of land as a site of friction and connection. She draws on colonial history, incorporating the 1783 Cedula of Population, which encouraged by way of assignments of land, an influx of French colonists, and their enslaved, to Trinidad. Jenkins offers vivid social commentary, complicating relationships and unsettling tidy lineages.

Together, work by Bowen and Jenkins produce a hybrid lens. With it, I see the valley of my being; my identity a hinging of my maternal great-grandfather from China, who would slip away to the forest to smoke, and my paternal great-aunt, whose warrior spirit was best witnessed in her practice of the African martial art of headbutting. In seeing myself, I imagine "the typical Caribbean person" who is "part-African, part-European, part-Asian, part-Native American but totally Caribbean" (Nettleford, 2003: p. xii). Looking again, I also see that time, in my late teens, when I volunteered to help clean a Pentecostal church, located along Trinidad's East-West corridor. I was reprimanded for standing on the altar dressed in pants – the legs of the garment taken as two parts of an irreverent diptych; my body deciphered as a scape or scene, a thing feared for the view it might offer beyond patriarchal vantage points.

More memories are evoked by a latticework of paintings and stories. Amílcar Sanatan's *Foots from Westbury* provides a window to an under-resourced community and the experiences of an adolescent boy, who navigates hardship while hoping a talent scout will see his soccer playing skills. His piece is a reply to Bowen's *Kneel*, a striking image of a figure on one knee. The speckled application of colour on canvas makes the painted figure wink, shimmer and move in a manner that keeps it from submitting to a viewer's attempt at fixing a gaze. It is a picture of kneeling as refusal. This resistance felt in the work is reminiscent of former quarterback, Colin Kaepernick's kneeling gesture, a political move carried out during the national anthem at the start of NFL games, in symbolic opposition to racial inequality in the United States. Yet, for me, more intimate recollections are perceived in the interlacing of Sanatan's vernacular prose with Bowen's visual vocabulary. I recall my mother's stories about her knack for mathematics as a child, and her enjoyment of reading comprehension classes. Such pleasures were aborted when Trinidad and Tobago introduced a high-school admissions test in the early 1960s – a feature imported from Britain's education system. My mother did not meet the age requirement to take the new exam. She was too old by a few months. She did not attend high school and her family did not have money to pay for vocational training, an option recommended by a teacher who believed my mother showed promise. Years later, she sustained a career as a pharmacist but her path was not an easy one. As my sister and I made our way through school, mom urged us to focus on our education. She would do the cooking, the washing and ironing of clothes. "Leave these tasks to me," she said. In managing domestic life on our behalf, I see that she was taking a knee, resisting anything that might curtail our potential for success in the "public sphere," beyond the private space of the home.

In Sharon Millar's *Mountain Cave*, a written reaction to Bowen's painting of the same title, she references the Cumaca cave tragedy of 1964. It is the true story of Adam Richards and Victor Abraham who went cave diving in Trinidad's Northern Range and lost their lives. Millar pairs this event with reflections on artmaking, and on acts of viewing artworks – offering a look at the way art makes significant intervention in daily life. A key point of entry for her story is the cave mouth seen in Bowen's image. Its dark, uneven depth providing a kind of Rorschach test that begs a discernment of figures, shaped from amorphous form. Between the contours of Millar's story and Bowen's blotches of pigment, I find my own doorway to a memory of one of the first art pieces I experienced as a child. It was a wood carving; a long, rectangular panel my father purchased and hung on the wall of our home. In fact, there were two wooden pieces: one an image of a lone steelpan player, and the other, the scene of a stickfight depicting two advancing fighters who moved to the beat of a seated drummer, chiselled out of the background. I was always drawn to the latter image. Perhaps it was the stickfighting arena – called a gayelle in Trinidad – that attracted me. "A gayelle is like a portal, a place to access transcendence," John Stewart observes (qtd in Riggio, 2020: p. 204). As portal, I often entered the space carved out in that artwork. I would look at it, for what seemed like hours, imagining the stick or *bwa* in my hands, hearing the sound of the drum, my mind and flesh transcending the physical plane of my family's living room, eclipsing arguments between my parents in the adjacent room. In the gayelle, I was a warrior engaged in my own battle.

The Snaring of a Swan: A Fable, is Kevin Jared Hosein's answer to the visual cues in Bowen's enigmatic image *Totem*. Hosein tells the story of a husband and wife exiled from a village, their marriage scorned for its unconventional coupling. The writer takes inspiration from the child-bride debates spurred in Trinidad by the case of Kumti Deopersad, who in 2018, said she had been kidnapped, but had managed to escape her captors. The 39-year-old mother of seven children later admitted to authorities that her abduction "was a week-long tryst with her secret lover, who took her away from her life of frustration" (Mohammed, 2018: n.pag.). Deopersad returned to her common-law husband, with whom she had a relationship since the age of 17. Amid public ridicule, local advocacy groups called for a recognition of Deopersad's story as a real issue faced by many women and girls who feel trapped in similar circumstances. Hosein summons this social context while also referencing Mongolian mythology, in which the swan is regarded as a totem.

In reading Hosein's words and Bowen's image, I think about notions of confinement and freedom. The powerful bird motif in Hosein's story elicits sensations of flight. In contrast, the coiled, knotted shape in the lower right corner of Bowen's composition suggests restraint. It is in their joint resonance – the verbal and the visual – that I remember family trips abroad, boarding airplanes for visits with cousins, uncles, aunts. This was the late 70s, early 80s. We always dressed up to travel. And, the outfit my mother selected for me, always had the same details. I wore a ruffled dress with the waistband tied in a bow at the back. Yet, as excited as I was to get to my seat on the plane, I was never comfortable on the journey. That bow's knot dug into my spine, and somehow, found its way to my stomach, making flight an uneasy experience, and getaways fraught with tension. How many women have felt – still feel – that kind of anxious pull? Nevertheless, my desire for freedom persisted. It would present itself in the form of dreams that saw me untethered, freed from the ground. I wanted to be a marine biologist or an astronaut. In Bowen's paintings, the fish-scaled tower, and palm trees twinkling like stars against the night's sky, are reminders of such ambitions. I see them too – water and air – in Hosein's narration of "gulch currents" and "the lightening chew[ing] through clouds like the flashing teeth of a beast."

Elizabeth Walcott-Hackshaw's *Sargassum Weeds* is a narrative vehicle for processing her bereavement – the passing of her father in 2017. While attending to pain as a state of internal transition, Walcott-Hackshaw points readers to the realities of external changes, specifically the growing problem of Sargassum seaweed invasions of Caribbean shores, attributed to such climate change factors as rising sea temperatures and stronger hurricanes. The writer references her memories of trips along the coast of both Trinidad and Tobago, in response to Bowen's *North Coast Road*, a painting defined by a long, winding path that makes transverse and vertical cuts on the surface of the canvas.

My interpretation of Bowen's image is that of a landscape's belly, an ultrasound scan of an abdomen that reveals the intestinal tract as a road through stippled tissue and crosshatched layers. When considered in combination with Walcott-Hackshaw's short story, I think about what loss feels like: a gutting, a hollowing, the way WASA (Water and Sewerage Authority) digs up newly-paved roads in Trinidad, exposing them, showing us their rawness. My first lesson about life and death – the way loss can come swiftly and excruciatingly – came at an early age. My parents' friends had invited us to their wedding. We celebrated their new beginning only to receive news, roughly a year later, of funeral arrangements. The wife and baby had died. The open casket image is one that still haunts me: a long box filled with flowers, the blanched faces of mother and child breaking through the petal blanket. They were not blood relatives but I was shaken by the sight, and a heavy sense of impermanence. I might have been seven years old at the time, old enough to read these events in tandem; perhaps too young, one might say.

In the book's sixth story, *Bitter Rain,* Portia Subran draws on her experiences at a Catholic school and church, and her interaction with Bowen's *Edge of the White Forest*, in which paint flashes like lightning tendrils around a tall mushroom-like structure. She sets a scene involving sexual indoctrination, along with questions about purity and transgression. Subran builds a narrative about a curious, shared experience among a classroom of girls. She keeps pace with Bowen's brushwork, her writing matching a melding of real and other-worldly realms that is unmistakable in his image. In this rhythmic flow between writer and visual artist, I add my own tempo. Bowen's pattern of white streaks and Subran's reference to "white rain – blocking out everything" take me back to the veil I wore for my First Communion Catholic ceremony. I translate the protruding form with the bulbous end, seen in Bowen's painting, as an eye with a long optic nerve – the sceptical eye I gave to my preparations for acceptance into a Catholic community of believers. As a child, I questioned everything I was being taught at church. Mandatory religious classes seemed devoted to diminishing my sense of self. The teachings suggested that I was sullied, "impure," and in need of the grace of forgiveness. To sanctify my soul I had to participate in the Sacrament of Penance or First Confession, before advancing to First Communion. I remember the priest asking me to confess all the sins I had committed in the past week. Nothing came to mind. What sin? Didn't he know that I was "working out my own salvation," heeding apostle Paul's instructions given in Philippians? So, I lied to the priest. He looked like he needed my confession more than I did. I fabricated a list of offences, then went home to my mother and told her the truth about what I had done that day. In my eyes, she, alone, had the power to grant my absolution. My relationship with her was sacred.

• • •

Reading these short stories and images – decoding the creole language they construct together – I am surprised by what my imagination, as light source, uncovers; what imagination, as actuality, *actualises* in a surrender of what I know about myself. My memories, washed out like overexposed film in the sun, now emerge under a black, UV light. They constitute the unforeseen. They are the unlooked-for of the black light void; a collage of emotions and happenings, re-membered sensory details brought out of their latency. Experiences present – there – but now illuminated in an encounter with self; a vision of self that is radical in its unpredictability. It is this incalculable element that enlivens this book as lavway. In this call and response, I deliberately make room for readers to enter, not giving away the particulars of each short story, and resisting an academic orientation toward exhaustive analyses of Bowen's paintings. It is a permission to see for oneself, and an acknowledgement that I cannot picture, with certainty, the interpretive outcomes for each reader. What is certain, however, is that each of us, in our participation in this performance space, becomes a storyteller, wielding the power to see and to say, crafting meanings and narratives, injecting unforeseeable imaginings that keep these artworks and short stories from the Caribbean, breathing, unfixed, open, ever-unfolding – a Caribbean always in the making. The stories that lie beyond glossy beachscapes are mine. They are yours too.

• • •

In the black light void you will meet yourself. You will imagine yourself, not in the mustard light that ramajays across the Caroni plains, or in the warm glow that limbos beneath creeping branches along limestone trails to Cumaca Falls, but in blackness. Your eyes will adjust in this different light, before finding maps, insights that can free you to shift your position, to alter the geography of your being. Like me, you must return to the void, again and again, knowing maps of identity are never final. As you journey with the work by these artists, perhaps what you will also find is that the images and stories are not foreign, that the Caribbean is not an exotic Other, but rather, a tropical place that extends to the loose, sandy shores of the self – part of the topography of your own life.

References

Baugh, E. (2006) *Derek Walcott*. Cambridge, Cambridge University Press.

Brosch, R. (2018) Ekphrasis in the Digital Age: Responses to Image. *Poetics Today*. 39(2), pp. 225-243. DOI 10.1215/03335372-4324420.

Döring, T. (2002) *Caribbean-English Passages: Intertextuality in a Postcolonial Tradition*. London, Routledge.

Froude, J. A. (1888) *The English in the West Indies Or, the Bow of Ulysses*. New York, Scribner.

Glissant, E. (1997) *Traité du Tout-Monde (Poétique IV)*. Paris, Gallimard.

Klein, Y. (2007) Lecture at the Sorbonne 1959. In: Ottmann, K. (trans.) *Overcoming the Problematics of Art – The Writings of Yves Klein*. Connecticut, Spring Publications.

Mayers, K. (2012) *Visions of Empire in Colonial Spanish American Ekphrastic Writing.* Pennsylvania, Bucknell University Press.

Mohammed, S. (2018) Kumti Left Home Again. *Trinidad Express.* Available from: https://trinidadexpress.com/news/local/kumti-left-home-again/article_5b7097d0-39b7-11e8-b1c1-d3de4340e0ea.html [Accessed January 19, 2022].

Naipaul, V.S. (1962) *The Middle Passage.* London, Andre Deutsch.

Nettleford, R. (2003) *Caribbean Cultural Identity: An Essay in Cultural Dynamics.* Kingston, Ian Randle Publishers.

Paul, A. (2006) Irénée Shaw: Gazing at Herself. *Caribbean Beat,* No. 77. Available from: https://www.caribbean-beat.com/issue-77/gazing-herself#axzz7mynWNMu8 [Accessed January 19, 2022].

Paul, A. (2003) Christopher Cozier. *Bomb Magazine,* No. 82. Available from: https://bombmagazine.org/articles/christopher-cozier/ [Accessed January 19, 2022].

Pemberton, R., Matthews, G., McCollin, D., & Toussaint, M. (2018) *Historical Dictionary of Trinidad and Tobago.* New York, Rowman & Littlefield.

Poupeye, V. (1998) *Caribbean Art.* London, Thames and Hudson.

Quint, D. (1993) *Epic and Empire: Politics and Generic Form from Virgil to Milton.* New Jersey, Princeton University Press.

Riggio, M. C. (2020) Playing and Praying: The Politics of Race, Religion, and Respectability in Trinidad Carnival. *Journal of Festive Studies.* 2(1), pp. 203-235.

Serpentine Gallery (2015) *Marina Abramović Trailer: 512 Hours.* Available from: https://www.youtube.com/watch?v=fDIO3m2W4AQ [Accessed January 6, 2022].

Sheller, M. (2003) *Consuming the Caribbean: From Arawaks to Zombies.* London, Routledge.

Walcott, D. (1998) The Antilles: Fragments of Epic Memory. In: Walcott, D. (ed.) *What the Twilight Says.* New York, Farrar, Straus and Giroux, pp. 65-84.

Walcott, D. (1974) The Caribbean: Culture or Mimicry? *Journal of Interamerican Studies and World Affairs.* 16(1), pp. 3-14.

Warner, K. (1982) *Kaiso! The Trinidad Calypso: A Study of the Calypso as Oral Literature.* Washington DC, Three Continents Press.

Leap into the void...

Edward Bowen, *Valley* (diptych), acrylics, mixed media on canvas, 96 x 72 inches each, 2017.
Reproduced with permission from the artist. Photos: Melissa Miller.

Hinged

Barbara Jenkins

A diptych is a painting or relief carving made of two parts, which are usually joined by hinges. They are invariably small in size and, if an altarpiece, were used for private devotion.

THE NATIONAL GALLERY, LONDON

I

The Lord is my Shepherd; I shall not want

The man tenses his bare toes against the grain of the wood, still warm from yesterday's sun. When he first built the deck, throwing it out from his bedroom to hang over the edge of the steep valley side, in that first thrill of self-satisfaction, he would secretly fondle close to his heart the delicious thought that the whorls in the grain of the wood under his feet, each raised swirl and curlicue, were his magnified footprints – that he had put his stamp, immutably, on this place, on the very trees that grew here, even while, as tender seedlings, their sap rising and the early fibres toughening and lengthening. Those saplings growing, maturing, erupting purest gold through the dull green at the height of the dry season, then flinging into the air swarms of whirling white winged seeds, that find crevices and settle, binding to this very spot with wiry rootlets, for generation upon arboreal generation, they were imprinted by him. And he, himself, existing way back then as a scatter of genes, dispersed among sixteen forebears, who were destined to be pulled forward in space and time towards the compelling magnetic force that was the eternally encrypted He.

No, it wasn't chance that made him. It was destiny. Nor was it chance that gave him this. All this. While Haiti was in L'Ouverture mode and Parisian peasant women knitted at the foot of the guillotine, those sixteen ardent French royalist forebears, lured by the promise of land and safety granted by fellow Catholic Spanish royal rulers of an island to the south, fled a French island with their chattel. Thirty-two hectares of land per white immigrant, man, woman and child, and sixteen hectares per head of slave chattel to the owner of the slaves, added to a tidy sum to be worked by the chattel and their progeny and their multiplied progeny's offspring. Yes. Twice blessed with land and labour, his lot was cast by higher forces. Neither credit nor blame attaches to him. Incumbent on him is the duty of husbandry, prudent management of his inheritance in deference to his forebears and out of conscious responsibility to those of his line yet to come.

The man surveys his domain. In the far distance, the main ridge rises. Unassigned, its greens mix and merge in random careless abandon, a fitting backdrop to what is in the middle distance before him. A sugarloaf, whose dun colours, mighty immortelles set alight with their orange flames, this cool November morning. Their shade protecting his cocoa. It's coming back – the glory days when cocoa was king, Trinidad cocoa, best flavour in the world – and he's at the forefront, rehabilitating his abandoned acreage. The single estate chocolate wave hasn't crested yet and he's ready. He's counting too on the revived mystique of coffee. The word pricks a sudden desire. He doesn't call for Carmen. No one, nothing, is allowed to disturb his solitary early morning reflective grounding. If only everywhere was always as calm and as peaceful as this scene is now. So often he finds that people disturb his vibe with their presence. They should be neither seen nor heard. Just do what they have to do and disappear. He prides himself that he can look after himself.

Sure, he has household help. Take Carmen, for instance. She practically raised him from child to man. Even though her useful days are over, she continues to live in her quarters. He knows what a little flat like that, fixed-up, would fetch in short-term rental along this coast. But he has chosen to forego that. True he's following his late father's instructions about Carmen's welfare – her family tied up with theirs long time. But it's also his way of looking after the wellbeing of the village people. Down there, Trou Anglais village is a whole integrated cocoa payol community, everybody related to everybody. He is only doing as his father and *his* father before him have done for generations. *Noblesse oblige* the great aunts call it. Working at the big house gives prestige to key villagers and in exchange gives him inside knowledge of what people are thinking, saying and even planning. A carefully calibrated barter that no amount of money could replace, he has frequently to remind himself when work is sloppy or a long weekend extends into a week's impromptu holiday, as they're wont to do.

Look at Jo-Jo, for example. Divali falling on a Wednesday, today, is a one-day holiday in the middle of the week. No sign of Jo-Jo since the Friday before and he knows, he knows like he knows that this barely risen sun will arc through the sky and set this evening behind a distant ridge, that Jo-Jo is using this day-off as a bridge to join the weekend gone to the weekend coming. And the boy not even Hindu! He knows that he won't be seeing Jo-Jo till the Monday after. No work, no pay, it's true, but the inconvenience? The arugula, kale, spinach, bok choy and mustard seedlings should be going in this week. Organic fancy greens are a thing now – everyone seems to be starting the day with a juice or a smoothie – and he's poised to meet the demand. He's got a whole business plan, from soil to stomach. Grow greens, juice them, bottle juice, chill, deliver fresh to selected high-end outlets: gyms, spas, health food stores, gourmet shops. Green Goodness. Mixed juices too. Mangoes and carambolas, fruit dropping like rain this season. Pomerac, pommecythere, sapodilla, zaboca. Everything always in excess. What's the hold-up? Labour. Can't get people to commit. Everybody wants everything too easy. If they not out fishing, they're tending their own little food garden. And the irony of it! He owns those plots of land that distract his workers, his *tenants*, from doing his work. At least, he comforts himself, he knows what *his* tenants are doing on his land. He can control or at least keep an eye. Lord knows what is going on in the uncharted places beyond. Seems like state land belongs to whoever wants to take it for whatever purpose. Big people, little people, squatting then legalising everywhere. Total disorder. Ah well! Coffee calls. Always best to know to walk away from what you can't control.

The man passes along the wide corridor on the way to the kitchen. There, on the wall, hangs a painting. Just looking at it and his irritation subsides. The work of an itinerant mulatto artist, travelling on horseback with the tools of his trade through the mountains, capturing for posterity, the estates of the landed. So said his father, who got that story from *his* grandfather, who explained that the mulatto artist escaped questioning and possible capture because emancipation had come and all people of colour were set free. The man has heard that the artist's paintings are now much sought after. It would be nice to be able to paint. Or even to draw, he muses. But then, why? he asks himself. That's why there are other people. To do what one can't or won't do oneself. Division of labour. The very foundation of civilisation.

This painting shows a view of the old estate house, an elegant structure of wood, slender pillars, intricate fretwork fringing eaves, a house full of light and air, open shutters, a wide veranda, set among the forest. The artist gives glimpses of activity: men and women engaged in cutting, stacking, carrying on their heads woven vine baskets filled with the gleaming brown, russet and purple cocoa pods – doing what has to be done. Glancing light falling on arching bamboo hints at the presence of a stream below. The man knows every detail of this painting. To him it is an icon. He would light candles in front of it, place fresh-cut flowers in crystal vases on either side of it every morning if it would not make him seem ridiculous or dotty to the servants. It is his talisman. This is his tangible link with the ancestral truth of his being chosen. Blessed thrice on this land. Not forgetting La Compensation – the payment from Westminster for the loss of property – the bodies owned by his ancestors.

Hmmmm … he will use that name *La Compensation* as his label. He could spin it that the estate is compensating for history by providing quality produce and creating employment at all levels of production. Yes! Key words for accessing government funding for the enterprise – *Vertical Integration of Production* and *Diversification*. Get some graphic artist to do old fashioned sepia copperplate writing on parchment type paper telling the story of cocoa and estates and process, put a picture of the old house, add some context, some romance. Wrap everything in that story – the juice bottles, the chocolates, the cocoa powder, the cocoa nibs, the coffee – toute bagai. People nowadays don't only want to know what they eating, they also want to get a spiritual connection with their food. Ah yes. Nothing like a cool early morning grounding for delivering inspiration. A shiver runs through his scalp as if at that moment the chrism of anointment is being pressed by the thumb of the Most High into the mole of his head.

A couple of steps further along the corridor hangs another painting. A woman in a yellow dress of a much earlier period. She is seated on a chair at a kitchen table, *his* kitchen table, where her elbow rests, quite at ease. A wide, white, broderie anglaise frill falling softly back along her upper arm, reveals a slender, graceful lower arm and a slim delicate hand supporting her chin. On the ring finger of her other hand, the right hand, curled over her stomach, a blue gemstone winks on its gold band. But it is her head that draws his attention every time. Framed by a bright red headwrap, her face is a smooth oval, illuminated by natural light coming in the room from one side. Her eyes, clear and bright, look out with an expression that he interprets as tolerant amusement, an expression that is mirrored in the secretive smile playing across her lips. As if she's sitting for the artist, only to humour someone else. She is at ease. Like someone who knows her place. Someone who knows her worth.

The man can't figure out why her expression in both face and body, her silky feline insouciance, gets under his skin. But it does. Who is she? Marie Louise, his father said. That's what my grandfather told me. The man didn't question his father further, but torments himself each time he passes by. Why did he have the artist paint a Black woman? Someone who must have been his slave? And place her here, right here, where he must pass many times during the day? He would like to remove her. Put her in some cupboard or storeroom away from the other painting. He would sell her if he could. She'd fetch a good price in today's market. But he can't. The two paintings came down to him together, as a pair. He's afraid that he'd interfere with his jingay and bring who knows what manner of retribution upon himself if he were to disturb the order of things as they came to him. No more than an irritated sideways glance, and he continues to the kitchen and the ritual calm of coffee this early morning.

He maketh me to lie down in green pastures

Sunlight sifts through the interlacing bamboo, scattering coins of golden light on Jo-Jo's upturned face. He stirs in his dream state, turns on his side, crooking his arm as a headrest. The sudden musty smell of disturbed decaying leaves penetrates his nostrils. His eyes flick open and he looks around, puzzled. It's broad daylight. He can't believe he slept so late. He staggers towards a tree to empty his bladder. He won't use the river like the others because he'd once seen a video of small fish leaping from the river, swimming up a stream of discharging urine and entering a man's penis. The very memory triggers a shudder mid-spurt. The boys, Charlo, Nobby and Rabin laugh at him, saying it's a fake video, but Jo-Jo won't take that chance.

He wonders where they are. Maybe they left early to go after the lappe whose tracks they found yesterday. Either they were very quiet, or he slept like the dead; he didn't hear a thing. He's sure they didn't have breakfast yet – no way could he sleep through the aroma of brewing coffee. Little point in going to look for them, he won't know in which direction they headed. Good chance of getting lost for a few hours if he sets out blindly. He hopes the others don't forget they have to watch where they going. Is not just cocoa and coffee growing inside here. Plenty protected spaces with plenty protected crops. He checks his phone. Seven already. No messages, but then the signal is weak here. Too many trees. Perhaps best to go down to the river, have a bath, see whether there's crayfish about.

He looks around for a tool – a sharpened bamboo stick or a knife – in the only waterproof space, the small tent where clothes and valuables are stored, but he soon realises that the knives and cutlasses are gone. He pulls on a T-shirt and sets off along the dirt path, a little more stiffly than his nineteen years should suggest. An intense couple of rain-drenched weeks building terraces on the slope below the big house, cutting and splitting bamboo stakes, weaving palm branches between them, then back-filling those fences with a mixture of soil and manure, left his muscles cramped and sore. If he didn't take a break, he'd end up broken, like his Granny Carmen, who spends her days in bed, releasing the exhaustion of seventy years work at the big house.

In the little pool below the cascade, his body is stretched and soothed. He could lie there all day, sun on his face, cool water around him. Count your blessings, Granny would say, if she could see him now. The river is full, but in this week of unseasonal Petit Carême, the water is clear. Schools of little fish, guabine and sardines, weave around him. The crayfish would be hiding under rocks – he'll get to them later. Right now all he wants to do is let his mind and body drift. He must've dozed off for it is with a start that he finds himself jostled against the rounded boulders of a natural weir. He knows this spot. It's not much further downstream from where he started. He'll wade back and check for crayfish on the way. He pulls off his wet T-shirt and knots the sleeves together. It will serve as a net and sack for his catch.

He is near the campsite when a loud bang and the crack-crack-crack of its echo ricochet across the valley. From a clump of gru-gru bef, a flock of parrots rises, screeching. Before the echo fades, a second and a third bang fill the air with back and forth crack-crack-crack for many long seconds. A volley of shots, like a burst of fireworks, follow. Then a silence, heavy with the weight of that trapped sound. For a moment Jo-Jo stands rooted. He sprints to the campsite, calling at the top of his voice, the names of the others, listening for an answering shout.

II

He leadeth me in the paths of righteousness

Near the Valencia River Bridge the traffic thickens. Smoke from open air cooking fires and the cacophony of a filmi and soca blast-off invade the Land Rover. The man winds up the windows, flicks the lever that locks the doors and punches the air condition button. Vehicles inching into makeshift verge parking, people scrambling and wandering about, picnic furniture, baskets, crates being moved, slow his progress. In a few minutes he is beyond that, on open road. His eyes dart from one wing mirror to the other. Nothing. A white Corolla is framed in the rear-view mirror. Old model, newish number plate. A roll-on-roll-off. He leans into the mirror for a closer look. Woman driver. Big sunglasses. An elbow resting on the open window.

He relaxes back into his seat, steps firmly on the accelerator, and turns on the radio... *Hospital with gunshot wounds. One is in intensive care. Two others are warded. Another man has been detained for questioning. Police are continuing their investigations. And that's all from the News at One. Stay tuned for....* The man fiddles with the dashboard buttons and turns off the radio. He searches on his phone, finds what he wants and ... *Jambalaya, crawfish pie and filé gumbo....* He turns up the volume to join in with The Carpenters... *for tonight I'm a-gonna see mah cher amio....* As he turns his body sideways to fling the phone on to the passenger seat, his foot slips off the accelerator, and comes down hard on the brake pedal. He is still twisted over when a loud bang jolts the vehicle and he is flung headfirst onto the dashboard.

What the...! He touches his head where it was struck, throws open his door and charges out the vehicle. The Corolla is wedged under the tow bar of the Land Rover, a fountain of steam hissing from beneath its crumpled bonnet. He strides past and wrenches open the door on the driver's side. The woman is slumped over the steering wheel. The inside of the car is sprayed with pellets of glass and gouts of blood. The crazed windscreen looks as if someone has kicked a football through it. The man shuts the Corolla door, goes back to his vehicle and calls his lawyer. He then calls the police and the ambulance. He goes back to the Corolla, takes pictures of the woman, her car, his vehicle, and their position together on the road. He goes to his vehicle and takes more photos. He sends the photos to his lawyer. He pockets the phone, walks to the verge and waits.

Yea, though I walk through the valley of the shadow of death...

He is still calling for Charlo, for Rabin, for Nobby when he runs, gasping, into the campsite. And still there is no answer. No sign of them anywhere. He knows where they'd spotted the lappe spoor the night before. He would go there and look for sign of the boys having been there earlier. A long shot, but what else to do?

From the site of yesterday's lappe footprints, a freshly cut path leads through the tangled lastro of a not yet rehabilitated cocoa estate. He knows his shouts are muffled by the layers of bush and trees around and above him, but calling for his friends is now a mantra, an affirmation that they are real.

He stumbles upon Charlo, lying face down on the path. Blood makes a bright pool under his abdomen. Jo-Jo calls his name, shakes his shoulder and getting no response, he turns him over. Charlo's eyelids flicker. His lips quiver. Jo-Jo tries to lift him, to make him sit up, tries to get him to talk. He holds

Charlo's face, squeezes his jaw, asking, what happened, what happened, Charlo? He shakes him more roughly, shouting, Charlo, Charlo! Hold on Charlo. I'm going for help.

Thy rod and thy staff...

The man's lawyer meets him in the inspector's office at the police station. The lawyer places his briefcase on his lap, opens it, and pulls out a printed sheet of paper. He hands it to the man. It is a statement of the motor vehicle accident in which the man's Land Rover, registration number such-and-such, was hit from behind at such-and-such a location by the white Corolla, registration number such-and-such driven by an unidentified female. There are photos of the scene of the accident printed on the statement. There is a print of a photo of the man's driver's permit and of the current insurance certificate of the vehicle. The lawyer passes him a pen and he signs it. The lawyer takes the sheet of paper and folds it. He opens his briefcase, places the folded sheet of paper in an envelope, seals it and hands it to the inspector who drops it in his desk drawer.

At the door the man turns to thank the inspector and asks, Do you know who she is? Yes, says the inspector. Driver's license in her purse. Maria Luisa Lopez. From up your side – Trou Anglais. You know her? the inspector asks. I don't think so. I didn't really see her face. She's OK? he asks. The ambulance took her to the hospital, the inspector says. That's all I know. What about my vehicle? asks the man. Can I move it? If you can drive it, take it, the inspector says. The wrecker will bring the other one here.

The sun is already going down when the man starts up his Land Rover at the accident site. The lawyer calls out from his car. Want me to follow you? Make sure you're OK? Thanks. I'll be fine, the man says, I think I'll go back home. Too late to head to town now anyway. He drives cautiously, retracing his journey of just a few hours before. A constant stream of traffic is moving in the opposite direction. At the Valencia River Bridge, he is once again forced to slow down. Stragglers of the day's relaxation are packing up, turning off sound systems, urging on tired children. Thin curls of smoke mark the abandoned picnic sites. Below, through the murkiness of dusk, the river gleams with trapped sunlight. It was round about here that he first spotted Maria Lopez's car behind his. She sure derailed his plans for the day. She shouldn't have been driving so close behind. She should have been paying more attention. Hit from behind is an open and shut case. The driver behind is at fault. His brake lights are working. She should have seen that and braked too. He is in the clear. Lost in rumination, he does not notice someone crossing the road in front of his car until, out of the corner of his eye, he makes out a figure sprinting to the other side of the road. In his wing mirror he sees the blazing fire of sunset silhouetting the diminishing form of a man, shaking his fist at him.

...they comfort me

The policeman is under heavy orders to get a signed statement from the young man within the hour. Where the gun? Over and over he's asking the same questions. What you do with the gun? Where you hide it? Jo-Jo does not answer. He sits there, across the desk, as still, as silent as a stone, saying nothing. He does not look up; he does not look around. It's as if he's in a trance. You run out the bush, phone police and ambulance saying yuh friend get shoot and two others missing. Now when we bring yuh here to make a statement you playing dumb. The policeman gets up and begins to pace the room. Ok, then. You don't want to tell me what happen, so I'll tell you what happen.

You and your friends went to take care of your business in the bush. Allyuh have a gun. No licence for the gun. I don't even want to know where yuh get the gun. That is a separate matter. When yuh there, something gone sour. Quarrel about the share? Maybe quarrel about who to do what? Maybe they accuse you of hiding some. Cheating them? Heads get hot.

The policeman stops his pacing and walks towards the desk. He leans forward and faces Jo-Jo directly. His tone becomes encouraging, sympathetic. Boy, it didn't have to be something yuh plan to do. Maybe was heat of the moment. Maybe they attack you with cutlass and you was fraid. Was three against one. Could be self-defence. Friendly quarrel get outta hand. Nothing else. Listen, I know what allyuh was doing up there. We been watching that field long time, waiting for the owners to show themself so we could make a raid. We didn't expect allyuh to deliver yourself to us so easy.

Jo-Jo does not seem to have heard any of that. The policeman goes to the open door, looks up and down the corridor and comes in, shutting the door behind him. He pulls up a chair next to Jo-Jo and speaks confidentially, just above a whisper.

Listen, I was young too. Did plenty foolish things. I was lucky that I had the chance to grow up without something like this happening. You have your whole life ahead of you and I feel I have to give you a help out, give you a chance. Look at what you facing – unlicensed firearm, shooting with intent, cultivation of illegal crop. I can see you feeling bad about what happen. Here's what I can do for you. We didn't find the gun. So we not able to confirm whether licensed or not. The shooting. It was an accident. Not so? Young fellas find a gun, playing with it, some kind ah foolish target practice and that happen. The cultivation. We know you is just small fry. Is Mr. Big we really after. If we charge you and make a raid, it will go public and he will get away. We don't want to jeopardise the operation. So what we left with? Accidental shooting. You and your friends all in this together. They not going to press charges. It may not even get to court. And if it does, magistrate will throw out the case. All you have to do is make a statement. I will help you. Look, I will even go now and write it for you. All you will have to do is sign.

Thou preparest a table before me...

The road is dark, made more so by the dense forest on both sides. He peers ahead, feeling himself lost and confused in what should be familiar territory. In the muddle of his thoughts, a feeling that something is not right nags, but try as he might, he can't put his finger on what. He brakes, slowing the car, pulls off the road and stops. He leans back in his seat, closes his eyes and goes over his day from the time he left the house on a whim mid-morning. The white Corolla behind him. Both vehicles moving carefully through the melee at the bridge. The car not too close behind him. He sees it's a woman driving. That makes him feel safe. He relaxes, speeds up, plays music. He remembers his foot slipping from the accelerator on to the brake. How far behind would she have to be to avoid a collision? At what speed? How many split seconds in which to stop? Taken step by step, which actions led to the accident? Where does responsibility lie? The man sits up and opens his eyes. He looks ahead into the soft enveloping darkness of a late-year Toco night. He turns on the ignition, does a U-turn, and heads back to the scene of the accident.

The Corolla is still there. He pulls up behind and gets out, leaving the engine running and the headlights on. He opens the front passenger door and gets in. He doesn't know what he's looking for, but he opens the glove compartment and pulls out the contents. Sunglasses case, glasses case, paper maps, notepaper, pens, lip gloss, sunblock, hand cream, plastic pouch with car insurance. An envelope falls on the floor of the car and spills its contents. He picks it up. Colour snapshots. He flicks through them. They're old; colours are changed, faded. A mix of subjects – views of coastline, mountains, and people. The interior light is too feeble to allow close attention to the photos. He replaces everything in the glove compartment and gets out. He notices that the front windows are down, not that it matters weather-wise with that hole in the windscreen, but... he goes over to the driver's side, turns the key in the ignition and winds up the windows. He makes to go to his vehicle, hesitates, goes back to the glove compartment and removes the envelope of photos. Perhaps he should take the car keys too. Leave them at the police station for the wrecker. He does not notice the shattered fascia, splintered hard plastic, sharp as knives, jutting out, in the path of his arm as he yanks out the keys.

...in the presence of mine enemies

Working late? The man stands in the open doorway of the inspector's office at the station. Yes. Overtime. It's not only vehicle accidents we have to deal with, you know. The man laughs. Praedial larceny too, eh? If only, says the inspector. Shooting. The man raises his eyebrows and the inspector continues. Yes. But it's almost sorted. He looks at his watch. And then I can go home. What can I do for you? The man passes over the Corolla keys. For the wrecker.

Behind the man, a policeman opens a door. The man turns at the sound and sees Jo-Jo seated inside the room. What's he doing here? He asks. The inspector rises and comes towards the man. He's the one with the shooting. The man is puzzled. That boy shoot somebody? Yes, says the inspector. We have a statement. The officer is going to type it up for him to sign. The man gestures towards the inspector's office. May I have a word?

My cup runneth over

You realise what was the plan? The man is looking intently at the poorly lit road ahead but his words are directed at his passenger. Read. He passes a sheet of paper to Jo-Jo, who reads it and hands it back. This was for you to sign. That you boys shot yourselves. He glances over at Jo-Jo. That's true? Jo-Jo stays silent. The man holds up his right arm, long slashes from elbow to wrist, no longer bleeding, but a livid purple. I have to deal with this before we head home.

At the hospital the man gets out. Jo-Jo makes no attempt to follow. See if you know anybody. The man drops the envelope of photos he took from the Corolla on to Jo-Jo's lap and walks towards the A&E. In less than half an hour he's back in the car, his wounds cleaned and dressed. Found anything interesting? he asks. Jo-Jo has separated the photos into two piles. The smaller one he gives the man. There are three photos. The first he recognises as his great-grandfather. He has seen enough photos of that ancestor in family albums to recognise him at once. But this photo is not one he has seen before. In this, he is carrying a baby in his arms. The second is of a young woman. He doesn't know her, but there is something about her that's familiar. Where has he seen that knowing expression before? The third is a photo of the hated painting. The man stares long and hard through the windscreen. He doesn't know what to think. He doesn't know how to think. He exhales deeply and says, I was in an accident today. That envelope was in the other car. He points to the second photo. Who is she? Jo-Jo lifts his head and looks directly at the man. Granny Carmen's mother. My great-grandmother. He points to the baby in the first photo. That's her too.

Edward Bowen, *Kneel,* acrylics, mixed media on canvas, 72 x 84 inches, 2017.
Reproduced with permission from the artist. Photo: Melissa Miller.

Foots from Westbury

Amílcar Sanatan

Foots come from a place where no man does surrender. His skin black like tracks gangsters run through at night. He live not too far off de main road where sun does shine up everybody galvanise rooftop in de mornin' and dazzle in little children eye. The same children who looking to sweat between two old Stag beer case or somebody beat up brand name sneaker from foreign. They always play next to somebody curtain, mattress sheet, or white shirt drying out on the line. "Not by de line! Go in de road," threatens the old woman with arms surrendering to gravity.

Is ah marching band of car horn waking up the whole village. Too much car caught up in traffic on the main road. "Yuh cyah fuckin' drive?" is a greeting. Noise on top of muffler noise fuming the thousand always-in-construction brick walls built over multiple Christmases, biscuit and Coca-Cola advertisement posters and unfinished walls of bright paint. The place pretty with colour. Drivers have their windows up because everything they see dirty lookin' and poor, but they not close enough to see the bougainvillea clusters everybody small house and shack find a place to squeeze in. Westbury Old Road is de same place Foots big brother, Jason, born, rob and kill a man. And is de same place he end up dead, face down on de road.

A yute man on a bicycle ride up on he and he partners by de parlour, next to where dem bad boy does run cards. The yute man shoot Jason in he foot one time. He start to run on one foot. He get shoot in he back two times. That day, three man end up dead on Westbury Old Road. Foots find out he brother dead before he even reach up the road from school. The whole village of Westbury run up in he cell phone to tell him what had happen, so he come home after forensics clean up the murder scene. People was still outside like they waitin' for Foots to walk up de road with he face red with revenge or he eye runnin' in water. But Foots come up de road normal.

"Oh God, every night is a flambeau," cried Mr. Robinson, the shop owner. He fed up sell drinks for people to light up bottles on the road like a walkway for the dead and their spirits. Foots strolled up de hilly road slow, slow. He walked like he know it have ghosts in Westbury. Everybody stand up there but their eyes never make contact with his. He ain't see nobody and nobody ain't see he. He reach home and see he mother sitting on the table with she boyfriend. He couldn't remember that one name. "It have some Chinee food on the table. Soy sauce in de fridge," Foots' mother said in a half-dead voice, spitting out chicken bones.

The newspaper reported, "Three Westbury Old Road Murders In One Day" on the headline the next morning.

• • •

Coach Aimey nodded to the visitors. He blew his whistle. "Throw it in fellas, come in a circle, come in," he said. The boys gathered around his built frame draped in dreadlocks.

"What happen Coach, game now start!" shouted Sugars.

"When I blow de whistle, I talk first." Coach Aimey asserted himself.

"Today, we have some visitors taking a good look at allyuh and how well allyuh does play the game. Everybody here could play but it have bigger opportunities outside that don't exist in Westbury. I want you to have the chance to take them. One day you could be the next Yorke and play like Ronaldo and Messi. Yuh understand?"

The boys stood quietly giving their coach their full attention.

"So them is scouts, Coach?" Jamal asked.

"Yeah Coach, I want them scouts send me Manchester in England. Meh face go be on all the billboards that lining up the main road, every cell phone and every pack juice they selling, is my face making millions," Sugars shouted above the boys.

"Aye! Sugars, shut up! The only scout you will get is the one to help you tie knot and go camping in the forest!" Coach Aimey replied dismissively.

The boys burst into a cantankerous laughter, pointing and shoving Sugars on the shoulder. Foots chuckled at the side of his mouth, all the time.

"Okay, let's go, let's go!" The coach's clapping scattered the boys into the field.

Running up and down, swiping chunks of grass with their boots.

"In the air! In the air!"

"Man on!"

"Look! Look! Look! Look! Look! Climb right there!"

For the first few minutes of the game, Foots hardly touched the ball. Sugars was dribbling and making long runs through defenders, showing off his skills and nimble touches. As he lost possession, Foots gained control of the ball. Suddenly, Coach Aimey called Foots off the field from play. At first, he did not acknowledge the coach's call. Aimey shouted, "Foots! Out now!"

He returned to the sidelines, step by step, collecting his breath, upset. The boys on the field were shocked at Foots' early withdrawal. The game came to a stop. "Somebody fuckin' tell allyuh to stop? Somebody hear a fuckin' whistle?" Coach Aimey screamed across the field. The boys began playing again. Foots arrived at the bench and sat next to Jamal.

Jamal leaned over, "Don't study he, he moving stupid dis mornin'. Don't listen to anything he say about fuckin' scout. Two chupid fuckin' white man with no camera, no pen, no paper, nothin'. He always selling we dreams." Jamal never trusted Coach Aimey. Based on what he heard, Aimey was a coach in Westbury Secondary School for three years. One day in practice, Coach Aimey boasted that he brought five school championship trophies to the school and Jamal had not trusted him since. Westbury Sec. was the fourth best team in the region and ninth overall in the Inter-School Football League rankings.

Jamal was the slowest runner. He was the least talented player on the field and the most regular player on the bench. Coach Aimey does give him ten minutes of play every match because he thought that is the most exercise he coulda get from him for de week. But Jamal show up for every training practice, and every game without a blink, and sat on the bench. He used to be Foots' best friend in primary school but he kinda fall off when they went on to Westbury Sec. Man like Sugars, playin' football, playin' cards and playin' games with gyal, is Foots new friend.

Is Jamal who give Foots he name. Before anybody know that Foots was de best footballer in Westbury, Jamal used to sit and watch Foots kick ball between two barrel on Coconut Tree Trace. Foots used to practice taking shots on goal for hours until sand fly bite him out of the dusk to return home before nightfall. One day, Jamal was on the bench when Foots was on the field sweating against some older men. Foots dribbled the ball, kicking it through Coach Aimey's football pardna Marlon and his veiny legs, breeding him. Goal! "What is your name, small man?" somebody asked in the drama and bacchanal. Jamal, shouting from the sidelines, "Foots! He have 'bout ten foot to score ten goal! Allyuh not ready!"

As always, Jamal spent his life at the side of events and because he had seen so much already for a twelve-year old, he felt he could speak on all life's matters with clarity. Jamal told Foots, since he small, that one day he would leave Westbury for something bigger.

• • •

"Coach, if you put me on again, I promise I would play better," Foots shouted, gesticulating with his hands in the air.

"No. I don't want you back in the game," Coach Aimey replied.

"Coach, I want the scouts to see me! Look at how much shit Sugars playing, Coach. You know I could do better than that fuckin' shit, Coach."

Coach Aimey walked towards him and said, "let us talk, son."

Foots reluctantly came forward putting his hand against his chest under his jersey. He turned once to the busy bodies of his friends managing the possession of the ball and breaking into each other's shoulders, thighs and rib cages to penetrate the walls of defence before goal. He knew that his sprints down field, ability to turn with the ball and take a precise and sure shot on goal would impress the scouts. He knew he could stand out among the boys of colour-washed football jerseys who were not as good as him.

He turned again to the coach and noticed a letter in his hand.

"You and everybody know Principal Elder and me don't see eye to eye nah boy. So when she call me out to talk about the team and 'give me something', I start to worry because I don't trust that woman for nothin'. Long story short, you can't continue to play for us this August during we training camp. You will be missed and I know you will do well." Coach Aimey explained and handed him an envelope. Foots tore the top off and read the following letter:

Dear Daniel Mohammed,

Congratulations on your breakthrough performance at the Inter-School Football League (ISFL).

I am pleased to inform you that you have been admitted to St. Christopher's College for Form 3 beginning September 2010. You will join our football programme where you will receive the necessary coaching and administrative support to excel on and off the field.

Admission to our College's football programme is very competitive. You are required to attend our football training camp from Monday 9th August 2010.

Please call 673-4825 for further information.

Mr. Patrick Carew
Football Coach

"Go home, boy. Tell your mother you going to a good prestige school now and you will get to play real football on a proper field with all the equipment and a full kit.

Watch dem fellas over dey, print washing off the back of their jersey. They have Air Jordan and Nike but they can't buy a good set of boots and things to make them go far. I know you didn't think the whole transfer thing would happen but God don't sleep, Foots," Coach Aimey with a smile on his face, gave him a bounce.

Foots turned to the boys ranting and running on the field with his open letter in hand. He still did not know what to make of his early withdrawal away from his teammates, the letter, Sugars still showing off with the ball, Jamal fat foot spread out on the bench, and the attentive blue eyes of the scouts.

"Coach, I want to play for the scouts. I want a chance to get spot." Foots begged.

"Boy, none of them scouting anybody here today. Dem is my pardna from foreign who waiting on me to finish so we could go and get some beers," he replied laughing, as he kicked together balls in a bundle by the gears bag.

Shaking his head, Foots walked away, leaving his taller shadow, Coach Aimey, Sugars and the other boys behind. "Wha' happen? Where you going boy?" he heard Jamal say. He continued walking off.

He text messaged his mother,

"Omw home.
I get chru wit ST Christophers for septembr
so I go start trainin dy nxt wk."

"Home late work 2 trips 2nite
Peas in fridge," she replied.

• • •

Foots' mother was 29 years old. She competed with the younger women for attention, winin' impromptu against the shop wall when the speakers reverberated through the old road and tracks rocked the night away. On mornings, she sat next to the radio – the morning show talk nonsense, Super Cat throwbacks, old dub, Vybz Kartel and a call-in prize for the furniture sponsor – and took about sixty minutes of her day to herself. She was as pretty as the clusters of bougainvillea surrounding the iron debris and old batteries from cars left to dry rot in the front of her doorway. She rose to the sound of mufflers vibrating on the main road from the early morning traffic cutting across to the city. Just like the mufflers, she coughs up some puffs of smoke in her morning ritual.

"It is what it is" tattooed to her wrist. She wore the green outline of a rose on her right breast. "The house light. Doh weigh it down with yuh spirit," she told Foots any time he slumped on the foam he slept on next to the stove where she made tea. The house have some more space since Jason gone.

Every day Joan driving PH taxi to pay back Mr. Kenneth one hundred and fifty dollars for the car and whatever else she make is she own. It supposed to be a rent-to-own situation but Joan working that Mazda six years now. If she make four hundred in one day, she make plenty. If she make two-fifty that was an ordinary Tuesday or Thursday. Every day Joan getting ready to work taxi dropping off school children, old people and fat people who taking up two seats for the same price, and people who head and back wet because they don't carry umbrella. She does reach on the stand first. She try to call people by name. She know everybody and everybody know she. And she know that nobody like a woman taxi driver because they will never get you where you have to reach on time. Joan does drive more fast and more reckless on the road because she can't let rumour spread that she is one of dem slow driving woman. That not good for she pocket.

Man always like to ride in Joan car, front seat. Foots don't think is because she does drive fast. She like it because it is a kind of reassurance that she not like the garbage, and other woman, that man does throw away all over Westbury. She does come home late and come in tired. Foots does stay up and close he eye quick when the door crack.

• • •

In the beginning of the school term, he used the money his grandmother from San Ignacio gave him to travel to school. He had spent one week with her at the beginning of August. Granny can't see too good now but she always lookin' out for she grandchildren. The money lasted a few days. From the second Monday in September, Joan turned to Foots and said, "what you need, on the table."

Foots dragged his feet through Westbury, head down, only lifting his head up from time to time to wave "good morning" to the elders. Dem old people, immobile with diabetes, some with stroke, and poverty, and always killing time on the shop front. Spots of them in de mix of yute men wasting time on barrels gambling, sun making them darker, colouring their bare backs to make them invisible at night. "Bright boy! Look at fuckin' book in he bag. He mother kick out he cunt again. Foots yuh house in dat bag or wha?" Sugars said, settling on the top of a blue drum. Foots put his hand in the air half-hearted, acknowledging him and his viciousness. "Don't take me on eh, you's a good one," Sugars called out, holding on the rim, trying to maintain balance.

Foots continued walking unhurriedly. Around this time, the other smaller, primary school children scampered through the sidewalks, jumping in and out, sometimes slipping down into the drain water, soaking their school shoe in filth. Foots crawled downhill, no lunch kit and no bredrin heading in his direction. People from Westbury cross the road straight to the secondary school. Foots does go left. To get to the junction, where he would get a maxi, he had to walk alongside the main road. He usually walked with his head down but every so often he'd see the actions of those who flashed by him in their mostly air-conditioned cars – children in the back seat, drivers stuck in traffic talking on mobile phones, and picking their noses in the rear-view mirror. And sometimes when he made eye contact, he could see and hear the subtle pressure of the central lock of car doors. Foots had curly hair and he short. He teeth have riders in front and he not a man of words so he mouth not accustomed opening wide wide. The only thing he ever killed was mosquito. He wasn't like Jason. What they think? He go beg dem? He go rob dem dat hour in de mornin'?

Maxis stopped at the bottom of the junction where conductors hustled and cuss out equally loud, and pushy drivers competed for passengers. Foots approached the passenger's window, inching forward. He had to psych himself up to approach a maxi. He avoided jumping in any vehicle with a driver's face he could recognise. He preferred riding in minibus with old men driving, playing soft music in the front, especially, gospel music.

Stepping forward, off the sidewalk, hands in both pockets, "Drive, you going Montpellier? I going long."

The driver, irritated with the comess of people squeezing into the minibus, rearranging bag and people foot and holding on to the head of his seat for support, rocking the maxi, said, "Yea small man."

Foots opened the passenger door.

"I have two dollars, Drive. I forget my wallet dis morning, Drive."

"Is eight dollars yute. You going up the road or no?"

"I have two, Drive."

As the maxi filled, the driver lifted the handbrake and simultaneously glanced in the side mirror to merge.

"Come in small man, come in front."

Foots hopped in and his stomach settled as the maxi drove off.

"Put on your seatbelt small man, police on the road today."

"Police not making money again so everybody paying ticket, ent Drive?" Foots said, making conversation.

"Boy, they need to make money yes, everybody feelin' it. This country gone to the dogs. Allyuh yutes only killing people and politician teefin' and everybody driving bad. Same ting. What the Bible say, happening now eh, small man."

Foots nodded, "True, true."

"All what in revelations happening now. Look how they find that woman body in a plastic bag in Vegas. Two small man get lick down in Ignacio. Aye, ah tellin' yuh."

"You have to watch out for yourself." Foots shared, listening intently to the driver.

"Boy, I see dey shoot up a school wall up Westbury where I pick you up dey. My big son tell me they now expel a boy from he school because a teacher catch de yute man hiding bullets in a napkin. A napkin? Ah tellin' yuh. Nothing new for me boy. Read your book. Forget dem yute men on the block, none ah dem could read and none ah dem want to. Government doing all kinda ting for de yutes but allyuh only studying big car and brand shoe.

"Look here small man. Is fourteen years I working maxi, I still renting in a choke up place, me and my two boys and I don't own this vehicle yet. Fourteen years, I paying loan – paying loan and have boys to raise. I not quarrelling eh because I makin' out good but I working my whole life. When I was in school like you, I only studying to make money. When you check it, I almost leave there chupidee because I cyah read no set ah contract but I could count meh money. School good for books but what you really need is common sense.

"De best is when you have de two: book sense and common sense. I telling my son, de big one, study hard boy. I waking up every day so you wouldn't have to work maxi every day so.

"I can't change the big one mind yet. He head too hard like all dem Black boy on de papers. He like music and say he want to be a producer. I tell him he could do all dat when he get he passes, but nigga don't listen.

"Anyway the little one writing entrance exams next year. I want him go a good school like you man."

Rejecting his compliment, "nah nah nah Drive, I not bright." Foots smiled.

Laughing and switching his eyes from the road, the driver replied, "I not bright like allyuh."

Listening to the driver's long talk was a small price Foots was willing to pay to get to school that day. When Foots arrived in Montpellier, he gave the driver his two dollars. And the driver refused to accept the cash. It was eight dollars from Westbury Junction to Montpellier one-way. Foots never liked to beg and he did not talk very much, just like Joan. If he had a choice, he would not beg on the return trip.

And every morning, he rose after his mother left. He'd find only ten dollars on the table.

• • •

On mornings, Foots saw Miss Penelope cleaning the classroom. She was a quiet lady, dark-skinned, with tight twists in her hair and a handful of greying braids to the front that she wore with pride. She knew all of the boys by name. "Good morning, Mr. Mohammed," she chimed in as she sang sweeping, "Lord, I lift your name on high, Lord, I love to sing your praises!" "Morning Miss," Foots replied. Miss Penelope cleaned up everything nice. Board clean, marker and duster in the corner of the teacher's desk clean. All she ain't clean is dem boys dutty sneakers that they never scrub since they start school.

It was only after the first month, Foots started leaving he bag in class when break and lunch call. In Westbury Sec., a bag in class is a gift for a thief. At lunchtime, Foots hanging out in the cafeteria and he is de only one with a bag. Everybody hand swinging with chocolate, a sandwich or Uncle Bil's oily aloo pie from the shop opposite the school. In the beginning, all the boys used to come around Foots asking, "What position you does play?" "You ever see a man get kill?" Dem glad to hear how he go play for the football team now but they was happier since he come from Westbury Old Road. One ask him if he have a gun. He never had one. It had one in the house though, Jason own, but he didn't tell them anything.

Foots was happy for lunch period. It had a certain timelessness, a strange peace and calm in the midst of boys making noise and mischief. Only athletes went on the field to play. Early on, Foots noticed that most of the boys on the football team transferred in or won scholarships to play for St. Christopher's, just like him.

In the classroom, he could rest he head, read a book or just think to himself. Sometimes, he sat observing the boys reading and practising problems and activities in the textbook. Even teachers sat in the classroom at lunchtime to assist the boys who asked for extra attention. He kind of liked the feel of the smooth polished finish of the desk on his cheek. Westbury Sec. was beat up and old. The classroom light flickered and louvres remained closed because somebody always combing hair, running a gamble or smoking in the back. Chair leg missin' from the last school war. The government bought new desks and chairs but they were all broken apart after the first year. Joan used to tell Foots, "poor people don't like nice things." Foots never believed it. He sit in St. Christopher's and see how nice things belong in a nice place. His mind does run on Sugars but he stop talking with him weeks now since he say that he was coming up Montpellier to rob some of the fellas for their cell phones. He know Sugars was joking but fellas from Westbury Sec. used to rob men to get a laugh.

Like the rest of the group in class, he too started reading textbooks during the break. But sometimes as the other boys in class were busy working on Math and reading *Men and Gods*, Foots sat to the back of the room, quietly, and faded into the wall. His mind use to travel all the way to Jason. Every time, it was the same daydream. They were both students at St. Christopher's, laughing about the ugly grey pants and maroon shirt uniform that he now wore. He knew he would feel better about his day, walking up to the form five block, seeing Jason in St. Christopher's colours with his friends hanging out on the staircase talking about girls and sports and, because they are in St. Christopher's, biology. He'd grab Jason by the ear and ruffle his curls, breaking them into a messier afro. Jason would turn to him and say, "I wouldn't walk out with you but we'll travel together," and Foots would give him a bounce, reassured.

When he woke up, he remembered that Jason was not good at all in football. And boys from Westbury never make it up Montpellier in maroon and grey. And he knew whatever Joan leave on the table for two of them would never have been enough.

• • •

Foots started getting tired of making up story in the morning to get to school. One time he told the driver he forgot his wallet and forgot that he had ride in the same maxi the day before. The maxi driver put him out. Foots didn't even bother to go in to school that morning. The day after noticing his absence, Mr. Carew, the coach and Principles of Accounts teacher, pulled him aside after football practice. "Your form teacher said you were absent yesterday. Is everything okay?"

"I good. Somebody just run off with my wallet on the junction but I won't miss any more days, sir," Foots replied.

"You have money for the rest of the week?"

"No, sir but I willing to work to make up for the money I lose. You know about anything, sir?"

Mr. Carew offered him a job to cut his lawn on the Saturday. And so it went fortnightly.

In school, Carew cussed out boys on the field in football practice and made jokes about seeing their mothers the night before. He tell a man, "You want to know where your mother was last night? Ask me!" The boy ran off the field and never returned to practice. He talked about Joan already too. He never met Joan but he shouted at Foots during a practice game after a sloppy foul throw, "Tell Joan to keep she fowl home, don't bring dat fuckin' shit on my field! Please!" In football practice, the boys call Foots 'Chicken Foot Souse'. Mr. Carew was known for not showing up for class and always talking on his cell phone during football practice. Yet, Foots took the chance to work for him.

Mr. Carew lived not too far from Montpellier, about a fifteen-minute drive from the school. He lived alone and the outside of his house had a broken down fence and hibiscus in the front infested with mealybug. Saturday come and Foots rang the bell on the wall. Mr. Carew came out by his entrance gate and let him on to the property. He showed him around, opened the door of the storeroom and Foots removed the lawnmower and cut the grass. When he finished cutting the lawn, he took a cutlass and trimmed the edges. Afterwards, he raked the grass into heaps and put them into garbage bags. For Mr. Carew's yard, he needed four bags but Carew so cheap. Foots had to ask him four times in one morning for a bag. When Foots dumped the bags on the pavement for the Municipal Corporation to collect, he shouted, "Ah finish!" Mr. Carew returned, always bare-chested with hairs, giving an appearance of a beast behind bars.

He drew forty dollars from the pocket of his shorts and offered them to Foots through the iron gate at the entrance of the house. But before releasing the cash Mr. Carew said, "Do something else for me nah, boy." The first Saturday it was to move some old fence he dead mother used to keep on the side of the house. A next Saturday, it was to trim hibiscus. Foots told him it was better to cut down the plant but Mr. Carew reminded him that he didn't ask for all of that. Another Saturday, he asked Foots to paint the two doorsteps red with a half-tin that still good from years back. This Saturday work usually lasted at least four hours.

When the job was completed, instead of taking a taxi to leave the community, he walked to Montpellier to catch a maxi to return home. He was usually tired and hungry.

• • •

On the last Saturday of November, after completing the job, Foots called out, "Sir, ah finish!" Mr. Carew came to the gate and said, "Alright, hold that."

"I woulda let you move some of the rods in the back but I don't want to get you too tired. We have practice game come Monday." Mr. Carew spoke chewing and spitting, shreds of sugar cane crushing in his teeth.

"Well sir, this is my last day with you for the rest of the term. Christmas comin' and when school close I'll be down by my grandmother in San Ignacio for the holidays. I wanted to know if I coulda get sixty dollars this time?"

Mr. Carew's face remained blank. His fingers gripped the iron gate more tightly as he said, "You raising price because it is Christmas? How you woulda feel if the grocery store and maxi man or the doubles man lifted the price for Christmas?"

"No, sir! It's not like that," Foots replied hastily. "You know how it is, I glad to work and ting, I just wanted to know if you had any work for me still, sir."

Mr. Carew told him that he would give him extra cash if he helped finish up some work around the house he had outstanding. First, Foots carried the four steel rods from the side of the house into the road for the collector. Then Mr. Carew asked Foots to paint the garage wall white. The wall was stained with football prints, dirt in the ventilation bricks and sheets of cobweb in corners. For hours, Foots laboured: dusting, scrubbing and finally painting the wall white as it turned to dusk.

"Yea sir, I done dey." Exhausted, Foots shouted into the house while he bundled the newspaper on the floor into one to throw into the bags of grass outside.

"You work fast there, boy. Alright, hold this." Mr. Carew handed Foots his cash.

"Sir, fifty dollars?" Foots asked with his hands and cash in the air.

"I go give you the next ten before the game, come Monday." Mr. Carew replied leaning forward in a relaxed pose against the iron, examining the job.

It was already dark. As Foots walked to the back of the house returning all equipment to the storeroom, he struggled navigating the darkness. He was tired but he moved with enough speed to leave Mr. Carew's property fairly quickly. Finished. He locked the storeroom door and began swinging his backpack over his right shoulder. Then, he tripped over the single brick at the base of the standpipe! Foots crashed into the concrete wrist first, cutting his skin. He heard the loud knock of his knees making contact with the hard ground. He screamed in pain as he tried to bring himself back up, "Oh God!" Mr. Carew ran outside, following the source of the cry and he saw Foots limping, holding up himself on the sidewall of the house.

Foots fell to his knees once more. He screamed agonisingly when he dropped his whole body weight on the coarse surface. Sitting on the floor, he leaned against the wall and gently cupped his bloody knee, patting torn shreds of flesh back down to the skin. His blood grew warm and the whole kneecap felt hard like stone. Mr. Carew ran to him and brushed some of the pebbles in his wound off with his hand too. "It's nothing Coach, it's nothing. I good." Foots said in denial. "Boy, I carrying you to the hospital. How you go fall down just so? All your knee and the side of your foot cut up," Mr. Carew replied, with one hand holding his phone for light and the other applying concentrated pressure to Foots' bleeding knee.

Mr. Carew lifted Foots into the backseat of his Mazda 323. Foots stayed flat, practising deep breaths, deep inhales and trembling exhalations. "Hospital not far from here."

As the blood ran and dried along his shin, he wished Jason was with him in the vehicle.

• • •

On Monday, Foots held on to the staircase handle and hopped up the flight of steps. He limped, one beat slower than his usual walk, to the back of the classroom. Joan could not wait around to see how far he could walk into the school's compound. She was impatient and grumpy the entire ride. "This knee not making me money." Foots did not complain because it was the first time his mother saw St. Christopher's College. He smiled slightly as he joined the queue of parents and hired drivers dropping off their boys in the morning at the roundabout before the school's entrance.

At lunch, he heard the stampede of boys run out of their classes to stand first in line in the cafeteria and Uncle Bil's pie shop across the road. Some of the other boys began rattling off the latest scenes of their favourite television shows. No noise came from the football field; the lawn was prepared and kept out of bounds for the match in the afternoon. Foots re-wrapped the knee brace around his left knee where the swelling had not yet gone down. "Aye, 'Gyptian! 'Gyptian! How you tie up so like one ah dem mummies?" The boy in front heckled him. Foots laughed and replied, "is because I hundreds of years old, yes. When I dead, bury me in a tomb of gold!"

Foots took his football boots out of his bag and placed them under his chair. Digging further in his bag, he drew his mathematics textbook because end of term exams began in two weeks. He felt pumped during the break, when the boys were busy eating food and information from textbooks, making music with pages turning and pencils slamming on the wooden desktops as they debated. Foots sat through the period, on his own, reading until Mrs. Ganness from the main office, entered the classroom, "Is Daniel here?"

"Miss, yuh mean Foots?" the boy closest to the door shouted, pointing to the back. She walked to the end of the classroom where Foots filled the corner with his inconspicuousness, curly hair and rank smell of Iodex, exposing a letter in her hand. "You would have to show this to your mother and she would have to come into the school after to discuss some matters," she said, handing him the letter addressed to his mother.

Foots hesitated for a moment. He opened the unsealed envelope:

Dear Mrs. Joan Mohammed,

I am sorry to learn of Daniel Mohammed's recent injury during football practice. I wish him a speedy recovery. Mr. Carew informed the administration of his hard work and effort during football training this term, and we look forward to his healthy return in term two, January 2011.

He will receive $600.00 for medical expenses and $1,400.00 in the form of a student bursary for his continued studies at St. Christopher's College for 2010/2011.

Please visit the front office and ask for the school's Treasurer, Mrs. Wong, who will provide you with further information on the details of the process.

Respectfully,
Mr. Richard Bridgelalsingh
Principal

Edward Bowen, *Mountain Cave*, acrylics, mixed media on canvas, 72 x 84 inches, 2017.
Reproduced with permission from the artist. Photo: Melissa Miller.

Mountain Cave

Sharon Millar

Two nights before the dive, each of the young men has a strange dream. The first one dreams he is at the side of a lake. The sky is not tropical. A certain sheen of blue suggests fjords and glaciers and he knows the lake is cold. High mountains on the flat water, doppelgangers of light and dark hinging on the horizon. When the snake slips into the water, his eyes follow the viper. A splendid example of dappled creams and browns, the rainforest creature glides under transparent foreign water. When it surfaces, it grows like a tree out of the water. The water holds, with not a ripple, as the snake raises to its full length of some twelve feet, stretching towards the blind sky. It releases its venom into the air, a fine spray of pale purple and orange that bleeds like wet paint on the flat canvas of the sky. He feels no fear. He has never seen anything so beautiful in his life. The second young man dreams he goes out into the sun at noon and loses his shadow. He tries again in the afternoon. Around him, shadows grow on the ground, spreading and elongating. Before him, the ground is light and innocent, ignorant of his solidity. In the way of dreams, time slips endlessly by and he is frantic. At the moment, he is sure to find his shadow, he wakes, almost in tears.

March 22nd 1964

"Promise me you won't dive."

"Really Mummy..." Adam steps around her, his dive suit over his arm. "It's perfectly safe."

"There's something about today..." She has her hand to her mouth.

For a moment the young men stop and look at her and then at each other. After a moment, Adam and Victor continue packing the car the way they have done many times before. Towels, change of clothes, sandwiches, cameras, flasks of coffee, bags for samples, string, tape, and so it keeps going. Between them they have generated a sense of excitement that is contagious. Every outing is an adventure. Something new to show and tell on return. Adam knows she's never liked the idea of the diving. Just the sight of the aqualung disturbs her. He has told her of the different worlds they uncover, the thrill of the unknown. You can't imagine the sense of freedom. It's like being in space. When next Adam looks up, his mother is coming barefoot across the grass to see them off. She pulls her dressing gown around her in a familiar gesture. How many times has he watched her do this? The morning is cool and fresh, another beautiful dry season morning.

"Where are you going today?"

"We wanted to dive a wreck off Gasparee but it looks as if that may not happen…" Adam trails off, looking over at Victor and shrugging. "We might explore one of the cave systems near Valencia. Cumaca. We'll see."

"Look," she points across the valley, "the immortelles are in."

Spots of orange flank the hill sliding from Lady Chancellor to St. Ann's. A morning gift. A good omen.

The karst landscapes of Trinidad's Northern Range are ripe for myth and legend. Caves, springs, valley systems, sinkholes, and grooved and fissured karrens all speak to different periods, from Jurassic to Quaternary. Legend has it that the sump at the end of the third chamber in Cumaca cave leads to other, more open, chambers. The stories have come down over the years. An Amerindian is said to have swum through and found the passage. Uncharted territory. The water that flows through the sump and on through the three chambers of Cumaca cave is the source of the North Oropouche River. This is the dive that Adam and Victor plan to do today.

There are experienced men in the club and they have taken every contingency into account. The cars follow each other. They turn off the main road in Valencia and drive until the road ends. There they unpack and assemble their equipment.

This is snake country, ten hidden mapepires for every snake seen. The walk is not difficult, if a bit overgrown, and along the way they pass acres of christophene vines staked and propped, wild costus, the remnants of an ixora hedge, an incongruous reminder of the manicured gardens in Port of Spain, and, everywhere, the ubiquitous balisier. Everyone keeps their eyes open for snakes. It is rumoured that the largest mapepire ever seen in Trinidad was spotted sunning itself on the giant rock outside the mouth of Cumaca cave.

The cave mouth is deceptively small. They are in twilight the first few feet in. Each man wears a headlamp and the beams of light catch on novel sights. It is the height of dry season but there is a steady current running towards the cave mouth. All are thigh-high in the murky water. It is not long before they are in absolute darkness, a silky blackness striped with the beams of the headlamps as the men turn this way and that. They examine their surroundings. The stalactites push down from the roof, marvellous and beautiful. There are stalagmites as well but nothing as spectacular as they have seen in other caves, where the stalactites and stalagmites nearly touch with cruel points.

Small ledges jut from the sides of the cave and this is where they see the young of the oilbird. Vulnerable with their fat and fluff, they call out at the disturbance. Above the men's head, the oilbirds wheel and scream, an eerie soundtrack like the cry of a devil. In the darkness of the cave, a curious landscape has evolved on the banks of the running water. Here and there, small saplings sprout pale and weak, reaching for light they will never find. There is much to be learned here but this group is concerned with the subterranean adventure ahead and so they push on. Victor lags behind to fill his sample bag. He has heard talk of the crane flies and beetles that are said to be found nowhere but in the depths of specific caves of the Northern Range. He collects as many things as he can find, rushing at intervals to keep up with the group. Adam is midway in the group, his body adjusting and acclimatising to the frigid water.

Large rocks rise up from the cave floor and require some navigation for climbing with the equipment. The rocks appear to be limestone, predominantly black but with some greys under an occasional beam and the men run their hands over the surface of the hard rock, the way they would touch the bones of a dinosaur. Oilbird droppings are like rain, and some of the men slip below the water to rinse themselves.

The passage between the second and third cave is very narrow. They wait in line to get down to floor level and slip between what is scarcely larger than a crevice. Less than a foot, surely, and the more heavyset men struggle to push under. The third cave opens like a circus tent. A wide pretty space with a high roof and sandy floor. The water here runs shallow and quiet before tumbling through the crevice into the second chamber. There are no oilbirds here but there are bats. The oilbirds' shrieks come to them as from a great distance. The third chamber is so placid and comfortable that for a moment it is hard to believe that they are over 700 feet inside the earth.

The men pull out the cylinders for the aqualungs, they assemble the line on a reel. It will link the divers to the surface, slim nylon meant to lie loosely on the bottom of the channel, the silt undisturbed. Everyone is excited, and the high roof, smooth water, and sandy ground give the illusion of safety. They all relax a bit, glad to be out of the murky water and away from the darkness and shrieking of the oilbirds.

"Let's suit up," Adam says.

Victor is catching blind catfish. The fish are white and blind, and they slip between his fingers like mercury. This is the fish that has made this cave important. He hopes that after today, it will be famous for the discoveries he is confident they will make. New chambers, new information on the source of the water, so much to be discovered. Carefully he fills his plastic sample bag with enough water to keep the two he has caught alive. He wants to examine them closely when he gets home.

"Come Victor. Let's see where we are going," Adam calls.

• • •

When the artist begins to paint, it's difficult to say whether he knows what will emerge on his canvas. He is working large. 72" x 84". Two mounds dominate the shape of the piece that will emerge. One larger hill in front of a smaller one. The smaller hill is symmetrical, mathematical in its precision. A green mound ringed with bands of violet and mauve. It immediately speaks of planting. Of using the land for harvest, and the effect is satisfying because the bands reflect both a constraint and an orderliness. There is also the suggestion of barbed wire, holding the hill. Nature contained. It communicates what he wants, and the artist is happy. But he knows, like everything he produces, the work will go out and people will see what they want to see. They will bring their secret pleasures and their hidden devils and lay them like an overlay on his work. But to him, that, in some part, is the beauty of what he does.

Now the other hill. When the artist begins to work on this hill, it's hard to imagine he does not know the story. When it is complete, he has painted, unconsciously it seems, the entire narrative. In the end, it is only this painting that can give some comfort.

· · ·

On Thursday 10th March 2016, the *Newsday* in Trinidad runs an article written by Martin Warwick Bermer: "Cumaca Cave Tragedy Revisited."

It reads, in part...

Everything seemed to be going as planned but of course there was no communication between the divers and the surface. We were not even seeing bubbles from their aqualung exhaust, and no doubt these were accumulating under the roof of the underground river.

We had planned on a half hour dive, at the most, with sufficient air in the divers' tanks for this and a safety margin. We all stood there watching the pool waiting to see them come back up, but time went by and after 20 minutes I was starting to feel some concern that they were staying so long. I thought I would see if I could feel any movement on the line so I pulled gently on it. There was some resistance but the line started to come to me and I remember turning to the others and saying, "they must be coming up!" and I continued to pull the line gently towards me, thinking that I was taking up the slack.

I was absolutely horrified when instead of the divers, the end of the line appeared with just a piece of white adhesive tape stuck on the end. Clearly it had come apart and we were seeing no sign of the divers.

Blur of horror. The rest of that day is a blur of horror at what had happened and at the need to go into the cave and bring out the bodies. We had then to set about the sad things which one must do after a death.

We attended the inquest, we called on the families of the two boys to express our condolences and share their grief. We had a plaque made and I found a place on the rock flat enough to accept it, and secured it in place with square copper nails hammered into holes drilled in the rock. Adam Richards' father, a consulting engineer, wrote to me at length to explain just what must have happened, showing me how the bubbles from the aqualung exhaust collecting in the roof of the tunnel displaced the water and took away support from the mountain which fell in on them.

• • •

"Do you like it?"

The couple are standing in front of a canvas entitled "Mountain Cave". There is a green hill on the side, wrapped in bands of symmetrical lines. The larger hill on the left is less structured. The more one looks at it, like those pictures that psychoanalysts ask you to look at – do you see a cow or a star? – the more the painting gives up its hidden figures and shadowy faces. The cave mouth is deceptively small. It is the dark centre of the painting that holds her attention.

"Do you see the man in the centre of the cave holding something?" She is close to the painting now. "Can you see it?"

He looks at it again. There are square lines above the cave mouth. On these lines are layers of colour. Lilacs, greens, purples, salmon, turquoise. He knows that he is seeing the vine-y, snake-y entrance to the cave but he feels this rather than sees it. And there in the shadow of the cave, the figure swims up into view. A ghostly outline with one arm outstretched holding a staff? A broom? She has stood back a bit, looking at the painting from another angle.

"Look." She points and reaches in to touch. He has to move quickly to stop her.

"Don't touch."

"Look at it … do you see the other figure? The one climbing the ladder on the right?"

The image is clear once he adjusts his eyes. A figure concealed as cleverly as a mapepire in leaf litter. A disembodied assembly of white strokes that communicate an ascension. An escape. You'd never see it unless you knew what you were looking for.

"Yes," he answered slowly. "I see it."

And suddenly he sees the whole thing.

When he gets home later that night, he pulls out the catalogue of the show and turns to the image of the painting. He sits and looks at it for a long time. When he has finished looking at the painting, he glances at his watch. 11.20pm. He has been sitting here for two hours. He stands and goes to his window. Nights in the depths of Maracas Valley are chilly, the air as cool and soft as moss. He is so tucked in against the Northern Range that it is an omnipresent force in his life. All the undiscovered caves. The labyrinths that run like tunnels under the surface. The puckered furrowed rocks and limestone and quartzite. The glorious sweep of mountain ridge is the last vertebrae in the tail of the Andes. He imagines running his hand along the top of the range. Up the peaks of El Cerro del Aripo and El Tucuche. Running his hand up like he'd stroke the tail of a dog, running against the grain, the bump of spine coming up under the skin near the rump of the dog. Past Monos, past Huevos, past Chacachacare. Over the Boca Grande and into the Paria Peninsula. The back of the dog.

He fetches the folder from the top left drawer of his desk. The latest cutting is dated Thursday 10th March 2016, but below this are many other papers. For as long as he can remember, he's been fascinated by the story of the divers. He was born in 1965 so he can't even say he remembers. Can't say why this story speaks so strongly to him. How did the artist know how to end the story? That has always been the missing piece for him. After the mountain devoured them, what happened? He wishes that there was some member of the families whom he could contact to show them the painting. What would he say to them?

There, he would say, there is the comfort and the resolution. They are not trapped, not even the one who was left under the collapsed mountain roof. They are there in the painting. The green hill on the right. See the christophene vines they would have passed? There is the old estate house, just visible. He digs to the bottom of the cuttings and finds his treasure. An old book given to him by a friend who had stumbled across it at a garage sale. A lined diary. Only someone who knew the story would know who was writing. Adam Richards had written about wanting to dive the cave. He'd written about his dreams. Victor had been having strange dreams as well. When he looks at the description of Adam's dream, the colours that bleed on the canvas of the sky, he remembers details of the painting. The foreground of the cave is spotted with soft droplets of colour. Oranges, purples, whites. These are details that give comfort and hope, and this is what he would show the families, if he could. Floating motes of colour that hover delicately, suspended in the forest air. They hover at different levels, clustered and separated, giving the illusion of movement and something intangibly beautiful and alive. The ground around the figure ascending the ladder is dotted with flakes of orange, fallen flowers of the immortelle. When he looks at the image again, more figures emerge from the cave wall. Like an ancient script giving up new secrets with every reading, the cave offers up a line of figures, all waiting to ascend the ladder. There are many paths to the cave, each one carefully contained in its own space and time. A winding path circles from the cave towards the ladder.

He puts the catalogue in the folder and returns it to the drawer. Before he falls asleep, he holds the image of the shrouded white outline on the ladder, head turned to the left, looking out at the pale blue triangle where the path ends.

...look...there...see...

Edward Bowen, *Totem*, acrylics, mixed media on canvas, 72 x 84 inches, 2017.
Reproduced with permission from the artist. Photo: Melissa Miller.

The Snaring of a Swan: A Fable

Kevin Jared Hosein

I

Her husband was at least thirty years older than her – she wasn't sure of his age. She could not recall how she met him or how she ended up in the village with him but she knew that for most of her life, he was there. He was a hunter. She knew him well, from the sound of his grunts when he chopped wood, to the smell of his flatulence after he ate boar, to the way his breath clogged his throat upon climax. There wasn't much else to know about him for he was a simple man. He ate when he was hungry, slept when he was tired, laid her down when his blood flowed right.

For the year she had spent in the village, her husband forbade her from speaking. A visitor to the village, a judge, had stayed at an inn the night of the Easter supper. He had brought his hound with him, and when the hound pounced on the wife and bit her on the neck, she cried out for her husband, who grabbed a rake and speared the hound through its gut. The wife was three months pregnant at the time.

Within the week, the judge held trial with the husband and wife. He had deemed their marriage unnatural in the eyes of God, the church and the commonwealth, and thusly banished the two on charges of heresy. The husband accepted the verdict without quarrel and they were given nine days to prepare their departure. The husband was a respected man and so the wife was staggered when no man rallied for his absolution. On the day of departure, the neighbours offered fruit, jams and seeds, which he accepted. One of the seeds was that of a rafflesia flower, gifted to him by a fellow hunter.

"What use have I for this?" the husband asked.

"A plague on thy pests," the neighbour replied.

Three men helped him cut and carry timber to his new lot. The wife packed her husband's belongings in burlap sacks and the two departed in a mule-driven wagon.

The husband spent a month carpentering the house, slat by slat. He filled the gaps with clay and ignored the imperfections, as he liked the way the light tongued through and licked the floor. En route, he and his wife gathered reeds and rushes from a nearby mire to thatch the roof and mat the floor. Two pitch-oil lanterns lit the porch at nightfall. From the distance, the house looked crooked and small, ready to be consumed by wild and wilderness. But he and his wife endured.

The house was less than a half-day's walk from the village. In between was a stretch of damp clay, a woodland and a series of gulches that flash-flooded twice a month. The soil was good enough for pumpkins, corn and lima beans. From these, the wife made cornmeal and succotash. The husband laid traps for rabbits and rodents in the woodland, speared catfish from a nearby estuary and took his bow to boar and deer that roamed the plain. He traded for bread. Eventually, he had enough to trade for two cows and a nanny-goat as he had a burgeoning yearning for cow's milk and goat's butter. The wife struggled at first to take care of them but soon, feeding and bedding them became the usual, as any routine.

One afternoon the husband brought home a mallard, its body lifeless and limp, a broken wing clinching his shoulder-blade. The husband slapped the bird's body on a wooden slab and skinned and drained all colour from its flesh. The image brought upset and alarm to the wife at first but she could not tell why. It was not the first time she had seen a fowl in such a brutal state. Still, she felt as light as a windswept parasol, fearing she would faint when she had to handle it. As she roasted the bird for supper, she could not keep her eyes from straying to its bloody jacket hanging at the window. At supper, she was not able to bring herself to eat any of it. Her husband had not noticed.

Later that night, she was awakened by the rattling of beaks against the walls. The sound continued until dawn. Because this oddity was no louder than a constant clatter of pebbles, it was not a concern to the husband. This persisted for the next few months. The wife wondered if the mallard had been some sacred animal. She asked her husband if seasoning and serving such a bird was an affront to God. The husband laughed in response, saying that if God did not want it killed, He would have turned the blade to butter before the killing strike.

When the son was born, a volley of birds rammed through the window at shuttlecock speeds. One of the beaks dashed the babe across the cheek. The husband put on his breeches, claimed his shovel and dug a hole in the middle of the house, at a spot concealed by a large keg. "Get back wife!" he shouted as he shoved her into the bedroom. She pushed the door ajar, watching as he retrieved a muddy cloth from the hole. As he did, a milky white glow formed in the corner of her gaze and she felt herself floating or drifting, as if the rooms were filling with water.

She came to the front of the doorway.

"Stay," he said, grabbing his axe. She had not noticed that her son was crying. "See about the boy," the man said as he bumbled to the back of the house and took his axe to the cinchona tree there. Each bough had long severed itself and at its top was a crown of flayed splinters, giving it the appearance of a corpse's hand bursting through the earth. He sliced a jagged hole through its trunk and tucked the cloth into the split. He knelt at its roots and planted a seed.

When he returned he said, "Peace thee. No more birds." He sat her on the bed. Looking into her eyes, he said, "The birds shall take no interest in thee as long as thou keep from this tree. Dost hear?"

And it was true. When she woke the next day a rafflesia flower, about as wide as the wife's arm, unfolded where the husband had split the bark. Its burgundy buds outjutting like the legs of a starfish. The birds dove head-first into the mouth of the flower, black and slobbering, their bodies vanishing into a murmur. The bones pearled down into the soil, where the grave-beetles chewed the remains. The flower stank of carcasses by the end of the week. By the end of the month, the wife had grown accustomed to the stench and at the end of the quarter, ceased detecting it altogether.

It was indeed done. No more birds. And the husband, the wife and their son led an undisturbed life for many years. Over time, most of her husband's face became beard, wiry like timothy hay, with his hair tapering into a scorpion's tail at the back. His body grew happy and burly, and his footfalls raised dust when he came back from a hunt. The son remained small – shamefully short and clumsy. The husband cut his hair often with his boning knife as he thought the boy looked like a girl when even a few strands went past his ears. He tried to teach the boy to skin rabbits but he fainted at the sight of blood and raw flesh – it was no different when skewering beast and hooking carp. The boy was more comfortable with the wife, his hands more suited to the hemming of garments and the grinding of pepper.

The man was not pleased with this, and in privacy, provoked the boy. He hit him on the scalp as an angler would take a priest to a trout. Alas, the boy was incapable of rage. The man decided he would have his wife bear another child for him. The child died in her body, and she almost died as well. After this, the man decided he would accept the boy as he was – as the boy made his wife happy.

The boy often left home to wander the woodland surrounding the village. On his sixteenth year, he met a girl in a white coif who was gathering wild berries and fennel. She was from the village and the daughter of a baker. She was small, smaller than the boy, but as lithe as a cat. She spoke carefully, as if there were sugar or salt on her tongue. They quickly became enamoured with each other.

When the boy met the baker, he helped him extinguish the furnace and stack the loaves. The baker taught the boy how to shape dough and whisk cornmeal. He was pleased with the boy's dexterity. The baker had not questioned the boy's circumstances, nor offered any conjectures. When the boy confessed that he was the son of exiles, the baker, being a bastard, sensed a kindred soul in the boy and told him that he should not be judged by the sins of his parents. The baker kept it a secret and he and his daughter agreed upon the tale that the boy was a waif. Unbeknownst to his parents, the boy was baptised.

When the girl visited the boy and his parents, she came with fresh bread, and pastries filled with crushed apples. An ambrosial aroma followed her. When she departed, the husband prayed longer than usual. In the night, the wife let her husband take her. She did not consider herself a callow woman. She knew her husband had entertained impure thoughts of the baker's daughter upon meeting her. She accepted this, as long as he did not act upon temptation.

The second visit, one month later, the girl inquired about the stench. At that moment, a pang of shame weighed upon the wife's stomach. The odour led the girl to the back, to the rafflesia and cinchona tree. She approached the rafflesia and as her gaze fell on its bloody mouth, she began to scream.

The wife went after her but as she came within a few steps from the tree, she was struck by a vision of her husband holding a knife over her. In it, her skin turned as cottony and white as a shock of lilies. The vertebrae along her spine curled and shuddered as a rattlesnake's tail would. A craquelure of broken blood vessels protruded from her eyes. She knew not if it were frenzy or prophecy.

At the same time, the husband barrelled out from the porch and held the girl from behind, lifting her by her breasts, and cast her to the ground. He did the same with his wife.

The boy arrived at this same moment. Never before had the boy felt rage. He ran to the girl and helped her to her feet. The wife was still on the ground, a brown hoop of dirt on the hip-side of her skirt. She kicked her feet to get up, prattling off an anguished apology while the father stood reluctant and reticent.

The son and the girl departed and did not return.

Though the wife still cooked, she did not eat for three days. She prayed with her husband, asking God for the boy to return. After a month, he ceased his prayer.

II

A year later, a letter arrives from the son. He and the girl have wedded and the wife is to bear their first child. They have taken residence with the father-in-law, the baker. He has been earning his keep as the baker's assistant, working to fill ovens and working to empty them. The father is pleased with this, as a baker is a man of sustenance, a man of timeliness, always well-respected among his fellow men.

A day after the arrival of the letter, the rafflesia withers. Within the week, the birds return. On some mornings, the soil is peppered with the crumbs of bird-bones. On others, the house is frosted, isinglass-grey with bird droppings. The mother learns to accept it, as well as the father. She scrubs the house every three days, wall to wall. The father replaces the roofing every fortnight.

One afternoon, a traveller, embarked on a donkey, stops before the house. Claiming to be a former employee of a trading post and an acquaintance of the baker, he tells the mother and father that their son is planning to visit on the day after the Sabbath, wife and newborn daughter in hand. Both are befuddled, wondering why the message has not come in writing. The traveller shrugs, replying that the courier may have lost the letter. The wife clutches the end of her apron while the father folds his arms, both in nervous silence. The father finally speaks, asking the traveller where he is headed. The traveller says that he has been exiled from the village for writing music that celebrates degeneracy. He is heading west to the home of a balladeer where he would receive tutelage as a fiddler.

The traveller has no answers to no other question posed to him.

On the night before the son's visit, the mother kneels and prays for mercy from the birds and their filth. Her prayer is in vain. At dawn, the house has been smothered with bird droppings. The birds perch atop the porch awning, glaring down at her. She snatches a stick of stovewood and flings it at the flock, causing them to disperse into a muffle of black towards the sky.

When the father wakes, he emerges, dull-eyed, wearing only his linens. The mother forbears from complaint. Her son is coming and she has to clean. The father grabs his cow-horn spoon and she pours him a bowl of corn pudding. As he eats, she soaks rags in water-pails mixed with sand and talc. She scrubs the walls and the slats. She uses a stepladder to reach the eaves and gables. The father helps her as soon as his meal is finished.

When they are done, the mother brushes the father's woollens and makes her way to the estuary to wash his doublet. The husband goes to the wood to check his traps. He finds a large ring-necked pheasant, still alive. He removes the bird and wrings the white on its neck until dead. With the bird's blue head slung around his shoulder, he gathers a few quail eggs before heading home. As the mother scours the muck off the father's doublet, she cranes her neck to the blanket of storm clouds above, grey as an ossuary. She stops her washing and mutters a silent prayer for her son to arrive before the rains.

When she returns home she stops in her tracks, trembling with fear, her gaze falling upon the bloodied jacket of the pheasant at the window. When she enters the house the husband is sitting at the table, whittling a piece of basswood. The body of the pheasant lies splayed on the wood slab and the quail eggs in a rattan basket. Remembering the mallard, the mother inhales deeply.

"Praise be," the husband says. "The bird shall feed all of us."

The mother knows she will not partake of the pheasant but roasts it still. Though the husband compliments the smell of its cooked flesh, it proves noxious to the mother. Twice, she takes herself to the back and heaves into a bramble. When she glances up, the cinchona stares back at her. It seems to scintillate before the cyclorama of the darkening sky, now gunmetal-grey. She returns to the house and finishes the meal, poaching the eggs with a mustard seed sop. It is evening by the time she is done. She lays the food on trenchers atop the table.

At that moment, the rains come. The boy best make haste, the husband says as he peers out the window. The mother muses whether the husband has said this out of fear for his son's safety or because he wants to eat. Grumbling, he takes to slumber. "Wake me when they come into sight," he says.

The mother pulls up a stool near the window, rocking back and forth on its cracked legs as she keeps her eye on the road. The gulches are already brimming with slush, flowing like tears along the face of the plain.

Hours pass.

Night has fallen but she is not sure how far.

Finally, she glances upon a speck along the road, illuminated by a thunderstrike. The lightning chews through the clouds like the flashing teeth of a beast. She rises from the stool, her heart caught between her teeth. She leans closer and realises the shape of a wagon, the mules trudging through the thick, turbid floodwaters. She hurries to the door, clutching her petticoat as an acrid blast of wind hits her. She jumps to the porch, swinging one of the pitch-oil lanterns to and fro, waving with open-mouthed joy.

When the wagon draws closer, she sees that it is indeed her son and his wife, drenched. Cradled and dry in the young woman's arms is a babe, swathed in linens, its cheeks flushed as if a candle has been placed on its gums. The mother escorts the woman and babe inside as the son ties the mules. Before anything the young woman apologises for their tardiness and that they have come bearing no gift, for they have not been able to salvage the breads and cakes in their wagon from the torrents.

The mother laughs and fetches a drying-cloth and quilt. On her way, she stops at the bedroom to awaken the father but he is not there. This strikes a discord in her but she quickly casts it aside. When she returns, the son has returned as well. The son, still drenched, takes the cloth to his wife's hair as the mother lays her grandchild on the quilt. Out of the babe's mouth comes a warm, cooing treble. The mother presses her cheek against the heart of her grandchild. The son takes his tinderbox to the fireplace and the room fills with light and warmth.

The mother, babe in hand, goes to the table. To her surprise, the food has not spoilt. It is still bulging with heat just as it had come out of the pot. She beckons for the son and wife to join her. However, they are not ready to eat yet. They instead sit at the fireplace with the mother on the stool behind them, rocking the babe to sleep. The fire etches a heart-shaped shadow on the wall behind. The son reaches for his wife's blouse and pulls it over her head. Bare-breasted, her body appears as a sculpture in an armature of embers.

Her eyes lock with the mother as the son disrobes himself and lays her naked body on the quilt.

The son penetrates his wife and they take each other on the floor.

The mother starts to feel ill. She leans forward, her elbows to her belly, babe pressed against the crook of her shoulder. It is not sickness, she realises, but jealousy. Never before has her husband held her like her son holds his wife. He has claimed to show his love by bringing her game and herbs and shelter, replacing each wet-rotted slat, patching each termite-bitten hole – but the mother feels guilty knowing that this love is not enough. And if one's love is not enough – is it actual love? The son's wife smiles, her teeth like moss, as the son brings her to climax. Her body gyrates, twisting into a corkscrew. The house begins to shake.

The mother glances down at the babe in her arms and sees that its neck has bent backwards. Its lustre has vanished and its eyes have turned black. She drops the babe and it shatters into pieces of enamel.

III

She'll open her eyes to find herself alone on the floor at the doorstep – the stool toppled beside her.

It'll be near dawn and the rain shall have slowed but will still be pouring. Listening to the husband's snores from the bedroom, the mother will slowly comprehend that her son, and his wife, and child had never arrived. It was a dream, she shall realise, a fantasy. Sitting at the table, her stomach twinging and twisting into knots, she'll not entertain relief. The pheasant shall have spoiled by then, snared and killed for naught. She'll toss the putrefying meat into the backyard, her eyes falling upon the cinchona tree, the birds on its branches roosted like lesions on a leper.

She'll step into the cold, approaching the tree on tip-toes. The rafflesia's petals will dip as if bowing to her. The closer to the tree, the more her body shall fight itself – not pain but a floundering similar to an urge to reassemble itself. Her skin'll itch as her pores open, each one the size of an ant's burrow. Her mind overcome by an incredible sense of desolation, taking her to the river, an unpolished memory of her floating down the current.

A bird'll fly to her ear and caw: The axe!

So she'll run to the porch and upon her return, seize the axe in her shaky fists and strike the blade into the cinchona bark as hard as she can. She'll never have used such force in her life before – she never had to. The bark'll open like a scab and she'll push her hand into the hollow. Immediately she'll feel a material as thin and light as chiffon. And she shall draw out the jacket of a swan, gangrenous with sludge, grappling with it as if it were a flailing fowl. The birds'll flap above her, enhaloing her, stirring the memories.

Her, a swan in a snare, and then her emerging from a tub of water. The man had had her splayed, prone, her feathers torn from her flesh. Whether it be of bewitchment or divination, she would've assumed this form of woman, with skin and fingers and breasts and hair.

The birds will lift the jacket with their talons and drape her in it. As it falls over her shoulders, heavy, muddy feathers shall sprout from her pores and her teeth shall twist into a bill, pushing every tooth onto the floor. She'll stumble about the house, graceless and violent as a goaded bull. A swan wading out of the hide of mother and wife. She'll beat a path to the porch and topple the twin pitch-oil lanterns. The house shall burn. The cinchona tree shall burst into flame, leaving only the tip of a lofty matchstick protruding from the ground.

Nestling into the floodwater, she'll let the gulch currents guide her, turning back to see her husband emerge, gasping like a fish before death. He'll take after her, a salvo of arrows and spears flying madly before him. But he shall never catch up with her. He'll trip over his feet, falling face-down into the water and atop his own blade, never emerging again.

Until sunrise, she will preen her feathers, pecking herself clean as the gulch's waters wash her into a pond near the village. She shall stay there, perchance for a fortnight, revelling in the daydreams of her son and his bride bringing her a basket of bread. And one day, she will forget she ever fantasised of such foolishness, and fly away.

Edward Bowen, *North Coast Road*, acrylics, mixed media on canvas, 72 x 96 inches, 2017. Reproduced with permission from the artist. Photo: Melissa Miller.

Sargassum Weeds

Elizabeth Walcott-Hackshaw

I came in with the Sargassum. Caesar, the fisherman, was on the beach preparing his raft to go out to his pirogue, *Sweet Bread*. He didn't see me, the colours hid my face which blended in so easily with the browns, mustards, ochres, blacks and sepias, all colours of the weeds. Islands of Sargassum were floating onto the shore creating hills on the beach, making it difficult for anyone to get into the water without being touched by the matted beds. It had been a long journey and there had been others with me but some got lost along the way and some got off on other bays on other islands, popular bays or deserted ones with names like Anse Cochon, Anse Fourmi, Bloody Bay, Pirate's Bay. I chose Caesar's Bay, at least that's what I came to call it, even if Caesar didn't know that it belonged to him.

Caesar's raft was made of driftwood and bamboo, bound together with old pieces of rope he had found scavenging on other beaches and up the rivers. His tee-shirt was torn, his tattered pants were cut just above the knees and were held up with cords of twine and rope tied at his waist. A long, scraggly white beard made Caesar look much older than his years, but his agile movements and sinewy sunburnt body subtracted these same years off of his sun-beaten face. Caesar headed out to sea on his knees, he was going towards his *Sweet Bread* with an old plastic bucket filled with bait, a paddle, and a look of quiet determination. His raft bounced like a light cork over the waves, just like the cork in that poem about the drunken boat. When he passed the thick islands of weeds he didn't feel me touch his face with the tip of my fingers, he may have thought it was the wind.

From my bed of tangled weeds, I could see the shoreline; it was a moment away but I waited just a little more before I decided to move onto the empty beach, filled with mounds of dried Sargassum that had come in earlier. As the tide began to change and the sea wanted to move further onto the shore, some of the weeds from my island began to kiss those already on the sand. My bed rocked as the waves moved in and out with a regular rhythm. Finally, the time had come to move from sea to land. By then, Caesar had disappeared with *Sweet Bread* heading towards the horizon.

Apart from the hills of Sargassum, the beach was strewn with piles of broken coral, driftwood, sea grape and almond leaves. Caesar's hut was nestled amongst the sea grapes. Parting the beach was a small river rippling into the sea. I was tempted to follow the river inland, up through the thick vegetation to its mouth instead of going into the island from the road. It had been a long journey and I was tired, not from fatigue but more from the anxiety of expectation. I was never sure what I would find on any island, each one was different and the stories from the islands were beginning to get entangled in my mind, much like these weeds of Sargassum. I never liked too many stories fighting for my attention, forcing me to become attached to things, people or places. No home had been my credo for as long as I could remember. I had learned long ago not to hold onto roots; unrooted, *déraciné,* was always better, remaining adrift, *à la dérive pour toujours.* This was our credo before we got to that cursed butterfly island. From then on everything changed; he broke our vow and almost broke me. Forgetting his promise, he found a home and decided to stay put (at least so he said) *pour toujours*. Before then he would preach to me (and I am sure there were many before me) in seductive tones, saying home was not a place, only an idea, home was something we thought we needed like religion, or Gods; the ocean belonged to everyone and no one, there were no real boundaries, the sea was always moving, just like us he said. But as we drifted closer to that beach all of that talk about being free like the sea changed quickly.

Still, as I look back (something I try to avoid as much as possible) I couldn't blame it all on him. How many times had we been warned by those who had travelled before us of the dangers of staring at anything too beautiful for too long or listening to sweet sounds for too long, slowly but surely we were giving away our powers. The vision before us on the beach that morning was something almost indescribable. A nymph so painfully beautiful that she made you want to cry, the way you cry when you hear music that breaks and emboldens you at the same time. We had seen many nymphs on many islands but this one was lying stretched out on the sand, half-naked, glistening and laughing. The light played on that body turning it to gold, then silver; some strange alchemy was at work. Some say it was what he saw but I believe it was the laughter more than that lithe body that tempted and weakened him. That laugh was a cross between a little girl's giggle and a whore's surrender; light and innocent yet voluptuous and open; it was shy yet inviting. If only I had been born with a laugh like that, with a siren's gift to possess anyone who listened to me for too long. I couldn't look as he made his way to the shore never looking back at me, not once.

Now I face these islands without him. He said we were supposed to be New World Crusoes, discoverers, real ones not like Christopher who saw a mass of something floating, looking like yellow grapes, so without imagination he called it *el mar de los sargazos*. There is more to this story I am sure, but dates, famous exploits, famous people flow through my mind like a sieve and everything goes back into the ocean. I have passed through too many seasons of seas, oceans, hurricanes, *ouragans*, typhoons and cyclones, to hold onto memories because I know that in time everything is forgotten. Those who still worry about these insignificant things have never seen roofs fly like butterflies in the wind, or walls of water like aquatic monsters crash down on villages, rush through towns and cities swallowing cars, trucks, buses, houses, animals, men, women and children, always children. You tell me what is really important after you see how quickly it all washes away. I prefer my island of weeds, my world within a world, carried along by the whims of the currents.

• • •

Every beach is different, the ones with tourists frying their bodies and drinking margaritas served by smiling penguin waiters, see our islands of Sargassum floating towards their shore as a sign of war. Our islands can look like a huge brown mass of land about to invade or sometimes we can be smaller, either way we are not welcomed. They assemble their troops: an army of tractors and bulldozers, soldiers uniformed in green overalls stand ready for battle with weapons of shovels and rakes. Their only aim is to destroy us as fast as they can. Some of us like the battle but not me, I prefer peace and empty ports of entry, secluded beaches, like Caesar's. I prefer to come ashore without drama, where it is easier to enter the landscape softly, like a shadow.

Caesar's beach was not far from the road, his surroundings were an almost forgotten place. There were no street signs on the narrow paved road. There were no houses, no cars, but the bush was overgrown and spreading onto the road. I waited to see who or what would come around the corner. I may have waited for hours or minutes, I didn't know. Breadfruit and mango trees, razor grass and palms with giant fronds of all shapes and sizes created a wall of green around me. There were no sounds apart from those coming from the beach. I could hear the sea rolling over the coral and pebbles, the pelicans diving into the water, the frigate birds quarrelling with each other and a light breeze rustling the sea grape leaves. Then the sound of a vehicle approaching; it was a white jeep with a young man driving and a woman, his co-pilot. I hopped inside and my journey on Caesar's island began.

The jeep was old and small but the two passengers seemed to enjoy it even more when it moaned and groaned going over the steep hills. At almost every turn the woman couldn't resist talking about the beauty of the island. He smiled and nodded in agreement but didn't say a word. They stopped at one point to take photographs of a fishing village down in a bay below. He told her to smile, she laughed instead, and he took pictures capturing her laugh, her wild hair and her smooth tanned face, the colour of glistening sienna. They were friends, lovers, travellers, and everything at that moment in their two young lives must have seemed golden.

Then, as sudden as a downpour in these Caribbean isles, without warning, the same smiling woman began to yell like a possessed spirit from some deep Inferno. It was near impossible to believe someone with a laugh as contagious as hers could produce a sound so guttural and demonic. Even her face darkened into a bloody burgundy and her large black-brown eyes reddened. She screamed, her body shook, she pulled at her bright saffron coloured sarong tied just above her breasts; it looked as though she would tear the cloth from her body.

He stopped the jeep, pressing the brakes with a piercing screech. Shocked by such a metamorphosis, he just stared at her. With the sudden stop, she held onto the glove compartment handle, her head almost hit the window, she wasn't wearing her seatbelt. *STOP! JUST STOP NOW! WHAT THE HELL IS WRONG WITH YOU?!* His voice powerful and threatening enough to startle her into silence. She muttered now like a child: *Why did you say her name? I don't want to hear her name, please never again, I just can't hear it not anymore.*

His expression softened slightly as he looked at her, *I didn't say her name* he said, *I don't know what you heard. Why would I say her name?* Now she wasn't sure that she had heard it. No, she had heard it, at least in her mind, but she wasn't sure anymore if he had actually said it. So, she stayed silent, adjusted her sarong and pulled her hair away from her face and into a ponytail. They didn't talk for a long time. It may have been hours or minutes, time didn't matter to me anymore. But I knew that just as the light had changed and soon it would be early afternoon, the mood of the car had been transformed into something else at least for the moment.

What neither knew was what I had done. I was the one who had whispered the other woman's name into her ears. I was the one who said ever so softly *Maria, Maria*. I could see that she was thinking about Maria even if he wasn't. Why I did it? Why not? Why should they be so happy?

The mood of the car had changed but the drive was still beautiful. We snaked our way over the hills, some turns opened up the dense vegetation like a wide curtain and we could see the sea again thickening the air with that familiar smell of salt and Sargassum. Snakes and Ladders, my favourite childhood game, up and down we went, just like my travellers, happy one moment sad the next, never quite knowing what was around the corner. My mind went back to Caesar, I wondered if he had returned to his beach or if he had gotten a good catch that day.

· · ·

We passed an old man and a young boy. I saw them, shadows on the road. The old man's face had that ashen look, like a grey veil over a black canvas. The boy's face, the opposite, brown and plump, just like the boy himself. He held the old man's frail hand and each one thought that they were helping the other; the old man walking his grandson to school, the boy taking his grandfather for a walk. The old man's back was slightly curved, his neck stuck out slightly, he reminded his grandson of a turtle or a turkey. The old man's eyes looked as though he was about to shed a tear, but in fact he was laughing. His grandson had just told him a joke about two boys in his class who were fighting over a piece of nut cake. The old man took pride in the way his grandson could tell jokes, or the way he remembered all the details of something he had read in the newspapers, or the way he held a cricket bat on the village grounds. So, on these mornings, as they walked towards the boy's school on the hill, they never ran out of things to talk about.

The boy's mother and old man's daughter didn't know that on that seemingly ordinary morning her life would be divided by a before and an after. How could she have known what to expect when she got up at the usual time, at 4am, still so dark outside, to pack her son's lunch and iron his uniform so not a single crease would be in his school shirt and two steel pleats would be exactly in the centre of his shorts – how could she have known what was going to happen? That morning at sunrise, as the three of them sat at the small kitchen table, the mother, her father and her son, sipping their warm cocoa and eating the warm buttered coconut bake, the mother giving her son the same instructions that she gave every morning: pay attention, don't talk too much in class, be a good boy (even though she knew he was a good boy already) – how could she have known what was to happen next?

The next time she would see her father and her son would be in that football field where her son used to play cricket on the weekends. It was a hit and run, just as grandfather and grandson were about to turn into the extension road that led to the boy's school on the hill. Some said it was a truck, some said a car, one person said the vehicle was white, another silver. Whichever it was, everyone remembered the bodies being thrown in the air like rag dolls and the deep unforgettable thuds landing on the savannah grass.

I had seen it all: the before, the during, and the after. I could still see the speeding white pickup (it was neither truck nor car), the look on the boy's face, frozen with fear, the grandfather's face seemingly unaware and the pickup speeding away, never slowing down to look back. As I passed that football field with my happy couple, the image of the mother reappeared to me, like a statue she stood over the two covered bodies lying on that field. What the mother didn't know was that every morning grandfather and grandson still walked to school chatting away, they were shadows on the road that only other shadows like me could see.

• • •

Their destination was a place called PASOS, the letters carved into an old wooden sign at the bottom of a narrow road leading up to a steep hill. The road to PASOS had more potholes than pitch but our jeep struggled along. The light was changing again, moving closer to dusk. My travellers were anxious to get to the place before all of the natural light was gone. At the entrance to PASOS, the dilapidated guard booth had an empty space where a door should have been, inside the booth had been overtaken by vines. They didn't see the guard but I did and as we passed, the old man with charcoal coloured skin and a well-groomed white beard, tipped his hat to me.

No gate or barrier stopped us from entering. Ahead was a fountain that I could see was once limestone-white with a small Cupid statue in its middle, perfect jets arching out of his tiny penis. But now, what my beautiful young travellers saw was a mossy circle of fetid water, a black, one-armed Cupid with a dry spout. He drove in slowly over the bumpy dirt road and we saw, scattered throughout the sprawling, overgrown property, wooden bungalows carefully appointed to offer each guest a magnificent view. *Imagine*, she said, *waking up to something like this every morning, that must have been so stunning*. She was right, without the colonising vegetation, the view to the Caribbean Sea from the bungalows had once been breathtaking.

The road came to an end in front of an entrance; it was an open porch with tall tree trunk columns. No walls blocked the view of the vast property. *This must have been the welcoming area*, were his first words since we had gotten to PASOS. *Be careful, we don't know if someone's here*, she said cautiously, because he had switched off the jeep's engine. *Who could be here? The place is deserted.* He got out of the jeep and went into the lobby area, the floor was tiled in a dark clay. There was a desk and two chairs to one side of the expansive room, a long bar with high stools for the welcome drinks and another area with a bookshelf (there were still a few weatherworn books on the shelves). All of the furniture was wooden, all fractured in different parts, an arm missing here, a leg there, and everywhere there were leaves, bat and bird droppings, as though the place was only swept by the wind.

They must have loved it here, he said. *Yes*, she agreed. He held her hand and kissed it with such tenderness that it irritated me; their happiness was returning slowly. Then she turned and walked towards the desk, drawn to it by the sight of the relic, a rotary phone. How had she not seen the phone before? She picked it up and looked startled; there was a dial tone. *Oh my God listen to this? It's working!* He looked at her incredulously, he thought she was teasing him. She held out the receiver but when he put it to his ear it was dead. *I know what I heard*, she insisted and he smiled and she became upset once again, her mood was forever changing like the sea's surface or a sky in the tropics. No more tenderness, no more holding hands, even the memory of his parents who had always talked about their favourite place on earth, a place called PASOS. And here he was with her in that very place where he felt held sacred happy memories of his mother and father. All of that was gone in a flash because of her moodiness.

Yes, I confess, it was me again. I simply had to stop these acts of love, at least for the moment. For now, they were both silent, quietly angry with each other, just the way I wanted it to be. She never uttered a word even though she thought she saw a German Shepherd in the bushes and a thin brown tree snake on a vine, and a man with a straw hat standing in one of the dilapidated gazebos on the property. This was all me of course giving her these visions from the past, I just couldn't help myself. But only I could see his parents sipping their drinks at the bar, whisky sours for them both, the mother in her long white island cotton dress, the father wearing a Panama hat, light blue linen shirt and beige trousers. Yes, they were elegant tourists from another part of the world who would leave all of their troubles in the plane as they walked onto their island paradise. Their son had vowed to visit this place with his own wife one day, hoping to find some part of his parents, in this place his parents spoke about so often, especially on their wedding anniversaries. He hoped PASOS would work its magic on them as well, to bring his wife back to him, start putting the broken pieces back together, moving past the betrayals, past the sadness of the last few years. It was dark when they got back into their jeep, in the darkness he held her hand again. She did not resist, and I left them to go back to Caesar's beach.

• • •

But by the time I had returned it was too late. Caesar had had enough. It was time for him to leave this beach, this hole in the sand. But little did Caesar know, the best was yet to come. The saddest thing was that I could not describe what it was like on the other side. And even when we sent signs, no one could read them. When Caesar decided to walk into the black water on that moonless night, naked as he was born, he didn't know that I was next to him: *Come Caesar, come* I whispered. He waded in slowly. Soon we would be lying in my bed of weeds, entangled together.

...in the darkness, imagine...

Edward Bowen, *Edge of the White Forest*, acrylics, mixed media on canvas, 72 x 84 inches, 2017. Reproduced with permission from the artist. Photo: Melissa Miller.

Bitter Rain

Portia Subran

Maggie Choon licks her wrists. She traces the skin over and over with the very tip of her tongue. She lies in a cot next to Jenna Stevens and Frankie, the air of the room clotted with a pungent mixture of vomit and disinfectant. Maggie catches the two girls staring at her, she's startled and almost whimpers, "I thought that if I could taste them, it means *they're real*." Frankie turns away, letting her head sink deeper into the camphor-scented pillow. She trails her fingers down the palm of her hand. She, too, has the strange red circles around her wrist. She counts them. Nine in all.

In the sick bay, in the immaculateness of white, there is a scarlet poster depicting the female reproductive system, with textured red plastic for the fleshy lining of the uterus, next to the sink is a step-by-step diagram on the correct method of washing hands, and there's a yellowed and frayed illustration of breast examinations. Hanging near the door is a miniature grandfather clock with a swinging brass pendulum, the ticking of the second hand echoes in the small room. Behind the shut blinds, Frankie can hear the wind sweeping over the grounds, gossiping with the foliage of the poui, scattering them across the fields, whistling through the gaps of the brickwork of the school walls. She expects the wind to build to a bellow, but it never does.

"How many of them came in?" Frankie could hear Mrs. Mangalee, the guidance counsellor, speaking to the warden from outside.

"About seven of them," the warden replies.

"At the same time?"

"This was during Literature class?" Mangalee asks.

"Yes."

"During the film?"

"Yes."

"*Romeo and Juliet?*"

"Yes. 1968 version."

A pause from Mangalee. "Just nausea?"

"Yes, but only Frankie *vomited*."

It'd happened an hour and a half in.

Romeo asleep on the bed, chest-down, he and Juliet naked as cherubs. Romeo's buttocks purposely angled to the sunlight. At this point, many of the girls buried their faces in their hands, some of them doubled over. Some of the girls let out grunts – Frankie still doesn't believe these sounds were faked or in jest. Getting the image back into her mind, the coldness returns, radiating from her fingers to her toes and teeth.

"We miss the best part of the movie," Maggie says.

"This school need to check their water supply," Jenna says. "My father could sue."

"It was probably something we ate," Frankie groans.

Maggie nods. "Garlic and eggs."

Jenna sucks her teeth. "Garlic and eggs, who you feel you is, Mrs. Mangalee?"

Maggie chuckles weakly.

"You know Mangalee and she husband does sleep in two different beds, right?"

Frankie's stomach knots up, as though she has been swallowing stones that morning, and she folds her body forward.

"Watch out. Frankie gonna spew again," Jenna says, pressing herself into the furthest corner of her cot.

No matter how many times the warden helps Frankie rinse her mouth, the acidic tang that stripped her throat raw refuses to go away. "You need me to call someone to pick you up?" the warden asks.

"No," Frankie says, shaking her head, her voice in a rasp. "I can walk."

"You're good to walk?"

Before she answers, the bell rings. The warden raises her eyebrows. "Well, that's that."

As soon as Frankie gets to the front steps, she crinkles the edge of her skirt as a lash of wind whips it upward. A metallic chill stings her gums. She tells herself she'll go straight home today – but still ends up taking the long route, towards Sweet Sip Café. The wind grows stronger, the closer she approaches. She has to stop and gaze at her surroundings – realising that nothing is moving with the wind. She cranes her neck to the sky, which seems to ripple like a loose tarpaulin.

The Sweet Sip Café is lonely, a little seedy, topped with a sapodilla-brown awning and with textured bricks, grey and muted, easily forgotten. Before she even enters, she can hear the chants of *Return to Innocence* from the old Yamaha CD player. The scent of coffee pushes against her as she opens the door. On the walnut-stained counter is a row of giant glass jars stuffed with preserved peaches, salt prunes and oatmeal cookies. In a glass case there's an assortment of sugar encrusted jam tarts, under a bell jar is a single iced chocolate cupcake. She rests her bag on a beige bar stool near a large bay window. At the very end of the counter is a trio of coffee machines, each of them labelled: Vanilla, Mocha, Chocolate.

"Vanilla, how you going?" the boy behind the counter says. He leans forward to meet her gaze, his smile revealing a row of teeth too big for his mouth. He keeps up the smile, looking down for the cups and stirrers. "You know, you're the only one who orders vanilla."

"My name isn't Vanilla," she bites the side of her cheeks to stop from smiling.

"It's Vanilla until you tell me your real name."

"Just give me my coffee." Frankie cannot meet his eyes.

She doesn't know the boy's name either. She knows the boy from church. He is in the choir, sometimes with a guitar in tow. When she first saw him, she knew she wanted to get to know him. She doesn't know his name – and knows better than to ask anyone in church for it. Stumbling upon him in the café was luck – mostly. Everything about him, she is simultaneously attracted to and repulsed by. She likes his voice but her stomach seizes upon its sound. She loses her voice within her throat whenever she searches herself for witty replies. She can't explain it. Yet she keeps coming.

She snatches the coffee just as he hands it to her and pays two dollars too much before rushing out of the café, rubbing her wrists, feeling the circles of callouses around them. As soon as she's out of reach, she bends over and vomits into the drain.

• • •

The next day, just as first period is getting started, the classroom door opens. And a voice cracks the low classroom chatter, "Francesca." The voice is smooth, dense.

It is Mrs. Mangalee.

Frankie clenches her jaw. She doesn't look up at first but she can feel the eyes piercing her like pins to the back of her neck. Finally, she turns to face the woman, her eyes fixed on her chest, on a gold necklace with a teardrop of raw amethyst that gleams in the frail morning sunlight. Her black straight hair is pulled into a tight bun, her middle path slices a pale line through her head. She moves and looks like a spectre draped in white. Her smile creases her face like a crumpled page.

"Coming?" Mrs. Mangalee utters.

"Yes," is all Frankie can say after clearing her throat.

"Ladies." Mrs. Mangalee nods to the rest before leaving.

Frankie counts the seconds before getting up and shuffling down to Mrs. Mangalee's office, which had been in an old prayer room. Unlike the other doors, it has an old, ornate pattern curling over from one side of the frame to the other. She grips the brass handle, and gives it a jiggle and a shove to open the door. The speckled paint is chipped near the inner edge of the door. Inside, a cracked bookshelf leans against the corner, alongside a column of cardboard boxes stacked to the ceiling. A metal desk separates Mrs. Mangalee from a wrinkled russet-brown office couch.

Mrs. Mangalee rests her elbows on the desk, her woven fingers interlock over her nose. Besides her open notebook, her amethyst pendant hangs off the branches of a miniature jewellery tree.

She gestures for Frankie to sit.

"How are you, Francesca?" Her voice rolls off smooth like velvet.

Frankie adjusts herself on the couch, her legs sliding forward from the unevenness of the foam.

"Francesca?"

"I'm good."

Mrs. Mangalee sits next to Frankie, and begins to comb her hair.

"This is for you to relax."

So Frankie closes her eyes. She listens to Mrs. Mangalee's breaths, each one matching the tick of the clock, as if each one is timed.

"How's your family?" Mangalee asks.

"Good. They're good."

"School? Your grades?"

"Um, they're fine."

She pauses, giving a smile. "Boys?"

"No," Frankie responds quickly.

Mrs. Mangaless gives a light chuckle, and tugs at Frankie's sleeve, pressing against the metal of the school badge. "What does this mean?"

"It's our school saint."

"What happened to her, Francesca?"

Frankie exhales. "She was attacked by a man. He was intending to rape her."

"And what did she do?" Mrs. Mangalee slows her brushing motion.

"She fought back to protect her virginity."

"And what was the outcome?"

"He..." Frankie swallowed hard. "He stabbed her."

"How many times?"

"Eleven times. She died."

Mangalee puts the brush down on the metal desk and it clunks.

"Stabbed eleven times with all her blood drained from her body. But past death, something was still intact. What was it?"

"Her purity."

"The essence of her wholesomeness."

Mrs. Mangalee returns to her chair. Frankie can barely keep her eyes open, her muscles are heavy and have forgotten their roles. She watches as Mrs. Mangalee idly pushes the amethyst necklace with her index finger, her gaze still fixed on Frankie.

"Every day, Francesca, all the girls here are in danger of letting their passions sway them. They're clear to be seen. Am I lying?"

The pendant glitters under the harsh fluorescent light, as it dangles from the jewellery tree. Frankie follows it drowsily.

"No, Mrs. Mangalee," she responds slowly, her eyes half closed.

"I'm glad we're together on this one, Francesca. Take care of yourself and have a blessed weekend."

•   •   •

After school, Frankie decides to take the long route – where the rain catches her, coming down from the scraps of darkened sky. The rain beats so hard that everything looks white. She pushes through. Is it really worth it? she asks herself. All this trouble just to see a boy? This boy whose name she doesn't know, who can't even be bothered to find out her name, who just sees her as another flavour on the coffee dispenser.

The café is up ahead, blurred behind the whiteness. She scurries up to it. There is no music. When she enters, there is no smell of coffee. Inside, it is stark and cold. The jars and bottles on the counter are gone. Behind the counter, the boy has his eyes fixed on the screen of the small television set to the back of the store.

"Need something?" he asks, his tone completely off.

"Coffee," she says.

"What flavour?" he asks.

She lets out a small chuckle, "I thought you knew?"

"Look. I'm busy."

"Vanilla," she says softly, her eyes locked on to the floor.

She sits near the window, looking out at the white rain – blocking out everything in the distance. No buildings, no poles, no wires, no trees. Her stomach twists, and a very slow tightness starts making its way around her throat as she watches him fiddle with the paper cup.

"My name..." she says softly.

"What?" he snaps at her, his mouth is pushed to one corner.

"My name is Fran-"

"Yeah Francesca, I know it," he gives her a toothed smile and then licks his lips. She looks at him, trying to remember when she told him.

He tips his chin to the door behind the counter, printed in bold black: STAFF ONLY.

"Come back here," he says to her. "I have something for you."

Frankie pauses, her heart racing, it's so light it can leap out of her throat. "Something like what?"

He laughs, "Just come nah."

She follows him past the counter and into the room. There's nothing there except a mop, broom and toilet – and the strong stench of urine.

"Sit here," he tells her. And pushes her back onto the toilet. He takes a step back and unzips his jeans. He grips himself.

Frankie clutches her skirt.

"Like it?"

She can't move. Can't breathe. It's as if boiling water is being poured into her stomach.

"Like it?" He's moaning like a ghost as he says it.

"Stop," is all she can say in drowsy murmurs.

"Like it, Francesca? Like it?"

"Stop. Please." Tears running down her face now.

His moans turn to screams. He falls backwards, splayed against the ground, the head of a mushroom splits his flesh, bursting forth from his body, shooting straight up to the ceiling in a pillar of blood. The walls crumble around them and there is nothing but the white rain. An antler of lightning rams soundlessly against the sky.

She's on her knees now, ash building around her legs, her hands bound with a fibrous cord that digs into her wrists. Blood crawls down to her fingertips. Her body jolts forward, a violent gale clawing at her face. The wind grips Frankie by the hair and tightens the cords around her wrists, she wails from the pain as blood continues to trickle down to her fingertips.

The violent gales drag her up a twisted, white-pebbled path, up a dark hill to a tree, bare, crowned with spike-like branches, its trunk wizened and mackled, beetle-black, sucked deep into the earth. Its gnarled limbs held its leaves, protruding petrified and fossilised. Frankie's gaze falls on a mushroom-headed structure with a pulsating red vessel creeping up its head. The petrified tree speaks to her, the voice of an old woman.

"Do you remember what lives there, Francesca?"

Her breath is shortened and the panic sets in. She turns away, remembering the boy and his moans.

"That is your sin. And look, there is your punishment."

Beyond the mushroom structure, there is the raging and screeching wind. The cyclone bursts up from the deep valley below her and whips into a violent storm. Nearing the edge of the valley, the white wind streaks down into endlessly traversing lines. The cold white wind eats of her face, and her body. She falls to her knees, crying. Just as it descends on her, there is a sudden hush. Her hair slowly drapes her neck, from being tugged, to stroked.

Frankie opens her eyes. The amethyst pendant dangles before her.

"You always fall asleep during our sessions, Francesca."

Mrs. Mangalee smiles at her, stopping the swinging chain with the edge of her finger. Frankie's body feels relaxed, yet numb. She puts her hand against her forehead, it was ice cold. She slowly pushes herself off the weathered couch. Mrs. Mangalee slips the chain around her neck, her arms cross at the wrists, clipping it closed behind her throat.

"This was a good session. Take care of yourself and have a blessed weekend."

Afterword...afterimage...

BIOGRAPHIES

Marsha Pearce is a scholar, educator and curator based in Trinidad and Tobago. She holds a BA in visual arts and a PhD in cultural studies. Pearce is a lecturer in visual arts at the University of the West Indies, St. Augustine Campus, where she also serves as Deputy Dean of Distance and Outreach for the Faculty of Humanities and Education. She has worked as the senior editor and art writer for *ARC Caribbean Art and Culture Magazine* and is a consulting art editor for *Moko Caribbean Arts and Letters Magazine*. She has also served on the board of the National Museum and Art Gallery of Trinidad and Tobago. Her research and critical writings about visual culture have been published in several art catalogues as well as peer-reviewed academic journals and books. Her essays "Reimagining History as Narrative in Contemporary Art" and "An Aesthetic of Survival: Denyse Thomasos, From Middle Passage to Colossal Endurance" are published in two recent (2022) art catalogues by the Art Gallery of Ontario. Her public scholarship includes a collaboration with the National Portrait Gallery London and the British Council for the *Americas IN Britain – Caribbean Edition* curated online exhibition project, and her work with the Pérez Art Museum Miami to co-curate the group show *The Other Side of Now: Foresight in Contemporary Caribbean Art*. In the midst of the coronavirus pandemic, she led an artist conversation series titled Quarantine and Art (Q&A).

Edward Bowen studied at Croydon College in the UK. He has since been living and working in Trinidad. Sans Souci village has played a major part in his work's evolution, allowing escape from urban life in Trinidad's capital city of Port of Spain, as well as a cross-pollination between the physical environment and his painting/drawing practice. He has participated in many solo and group exhibitions in the Caribbean and Sao Paulo. Recent solo exhibitions at Y Art Gallery, Trinidad, include *Stories*, 2017, *Heds,* 2019 and *The Rainwater Paintings*, 2022. Bowen often uses acrylic paint, ballpoint pen, marker, graphite, charcoal, and more on canvas – letting his experience and the present moment collide into complex layers, patterns, scribblings. In his words, "pushing surfaces routinely to oblivion."

Kevin Jared Hosein was born and raised in Chaguanas, Trinidad and Tobago. He is a two-time winner of the Commonwealth Short Story Prize for the Caribbean region. He has published three books: *The Beast of Kukuyo* (winner of a CODE Burt Award for Young Adult Literature), *The Repenters* (longlisted for the International Dublin Literary Prize and OCM Bocas Prize), and *Littletown Secrets*. His writings have been featured in numerous anthologies and outlets, including *Lightspeed* Magazine, *Wasafiri* and BBC Radio 4. His newest novel, *Hungry Ghosts*, will be published in 2023 by Bloomsbury (UK and Commonwealth) and Ecco (North America).

Barbara Jenkins is a Trinidadian writer who, after a lifetime as a geography teacher, came to writing in her late sixties. Her short stories have won awards at *Wasafiri*, *Small Axe*, *The Caribbean Writer*, and the Commonwealth Short Story (Caribbean Region), among others. She was the inaugural British Council International writer-in-residence at the Small Wonder Short Story Festival, Charleston, England, and the recipient of the Bocas Lit Fest's Hollick Arvon Caribbean Writers Prize for fiction. Her book *Sic Transit Wagon* was awarded the Guyana Prize for Literature, and *De Rightest Place* was shortlisted for The Royal Society of Literature Christopher Bland Prize. *The Stranger Who Was Myself*, a memoir of her early life, is her third book.

Sharon Millar is a Trinidadian writer. In 2012, she was one of the NGC Bocas Lit Festival's New Talent Showcase writers. In the same year, she was awarded the Small Axe Short Fiction Award, and her short story *Friend*s was shortlisted for the Commonwealth Short Story Prize. In 2013, she was awarded the Commonwealth Short Story Prize for *The Whale Hou*se and was nominated for the Bocas Lit Fest's Hollick Arvon Caribbean Writers Prize for fiction. In 2015, she published her first collection of short stories *The Whale House and other stories* (Peepal Tree Press). In the same year her article *Mermen Come Calling* was published in the New York Times, winning a CTO Travel Media Award in 2016. In 2016, her collection *The Whale House and other stories* was longlisted for the OCM Bocas Prize for Caribbean Literature in the fiction category.

Her stories have been anthologised in *Pepperpot: Best New Stories from the Caribbean* (Akashic Books), *Thicker than Water, A New Anthology of Caribbean Writing* (Peekash Press 2018), and *The Peepal Tree Book of Contemporary Caribbean Short Stories* (Peepal Tree 2018). Her work has also appeared in *Granta*, *The Manchester Review*, *Small Axe*, *WomanSpeak*, *Griffith Review*, *PREE*, and other publications. Millar holds an MFA in Creative Writing (2012) from Lesley University. She has been a visiting lecturer at the Sierra Nevada Low Residency program and has taught creative writing at the University of the West Indies, St. Augustine Campus. She currently lives and works in Trinidad and is at work on her first novel.

Amílcar Peter Sanatan is a PhD candidate in Cultural Studies at The University of the West Indies, St. Augustine Campus. His poetry has appeared in Caribbean and international literary magazines. In 2020, he won the Bridget Jones Caribbean Arts Award for poetry, and his creative non-fiction was shortlisted for the Bocas Lit Fest's Johnson and Amoy Achong Caribbean Writers Prize. Sanatan has performed spoken word and coordinated open mics in Trinidad and Tobago for over a decade.

Portia Subran is a Trinidadian writer and artist. She is the winner of the 2019 Cecile de Jongh Literary Prize from *The Caribbean Writer*, and the 2016 Small Axe Literary Short Story Competition. She is a finalist for the 2022 BCLF Short Fiction Story Contest, and was longlisted for the Bocas Lit Fest's Johnson and Amoy Achong Caribbean Writers Prize for fiction (2019). Her work has been published in *PREE Lit Magazine*, *Jewels of the Caribbean*, Akashic Books' *Duppy Thursday* Online Flash Fiction Series, *Small Axe: A Caribbean Journal of Criticism*, *New Worlds, Old Ways: Speculative Tales from the Caribbean*, and *The Caribbean Writer*.

Elizabeth Walcott-Hackshaw was born in Trinidad and is Professor of French Literature and Creative Writing at The University of the West Indies, St. Augustine Campus. She has authored and coedited 8 books, including *Border Crossings: A Trilingual Anthology of Caribbean Women Writers, Caribbean Research: Literature, Discourse and Culture, Echoes of the Haitian Revolution 1804-2004* and *Reinterpreting the Haitian Revolution and its Cultural Aftershocks (1804-2004)*. Apart from her scholarly books, essays and articles, she has also published creative works. *Four Taxis Facing North*, her first collection of short stories, published in 2007, was considered one of the best works of 2007 by the *Caribbean Review of Books*. *Four Taxis* has been translated into Italian and French. Her first novel, *Mrs. B*, published by Peepal Tree Press, was shortlisted for the "Best Book of Fiction" in The Guyana Prize for Literature Award for 2014. Her most recent work on *Aimé Césaire* was an Award-Winning Finalist in the Biography category of the 2022 International Book Awards. Her short stories have been widely translated and anthologised. Walcott-Hackshaw assumed the Deanship of the Faculty of Humanities and Education in August of 2022. She presently lives in the Santa Cruz Valley with her family and is working on a collection of essays, and another collection of short stories.